COFFIN RIDERS

JAMES W. BODDEN

N

NECRO PUBLICATIONS
— 2015 —

FIRST EDITION TRADE PAPERBACK

COFFIN RIDERS © 2015 by James W. Bodden
Cover art © 2015 Erik Wilson

This edition 2015 © Necro Publications

LCCN: 2015903350

ISBN: 978-1-939065-74-2

Book design & typesetting:
David G. Barnett
www.fatcatgraphicdesign.com

Assistant editors:
Amanda Baird

Necro Publications
5139 Maxon Terrace, Sanford, FL 32771
necropublications.com

Printed in the United States of America

ACKNOWLEDGEMENTS

A special thanks to David Barnett, and the Necro team for exhuming *Coffin Riders* out from six feet under.

DEDICATION

To Mario.

CHAPTER ONE

THE DROP

She calls my name like an invitation, "Bloom."

I dip into the tub and join her. Lorraine's skin smokes with the heat. She wades in the water on all fours, only the top of her shoulders and the eyes visible through the drifting suds and bubbles. My girl slithers right on top of me. A trail of red hearts runs down the stretch of her jugular. The vein throbs, bloated, thick with blood. I suck on her neck, and feel her heartbeat thump against my tongue.

Lorraine shudders. She throws back her head and moans. Sweat drips down her body, and her makeup melts with it. That pretty, made-up face of hers starts to ebb away and slip off her head. Black circles smear around her eyes.

She says it's almost time.

I sink my head into the water, and come back for air. The candles on the edge of the tub flicker around me. I play with the wicks, but don't feel any pain from the fire. The candlelight casts shadows, thick prison bars striped over my body.

"This is between you and me," she says. "Nobody else can share this moment. It's for us alone."

She clutches my hand on the gun, and closes my fingers over the handle.

The revolver's seen better days. Its front sight looks crooked. The grip's held together with nothing but duct tape. Even the cylinder has a trick to it. You have to roll it back and forth like a combination lock—four clicks down, then one full turn until the ratchet sticks.

I slot two bullets inside the chamber, "One for you, and one for me."

Lorraine's hands guide mine. She stiffens my grip. Shushes into my ear. Stops me from shaking. We cock the gun together, pull back on the hammer, and watch the cylinder turn. I shudder when it loads.

One last shared moment. She looks good half-floating in the tub with me. Her body is a tight fit, and even sexier covered in suds. Lorraine slicks her yellow hair and winks at me before sloshing back into the smoking water.

"See you soon," she says.

My blood goes hot. A dark cloud swirls into a storm inside my guts. Electricity sparks around my grip on the gun. I can't help but get a thrill out of this—something close to the rush of stealing.

A smile cuts across my face as I deep throat the barrel, and pull the trigger.

The back of my head splatters all over the porcelain. The rest of my body dunks into the water. I sink to the bottom of the tub for what seems like nautical miles. Currents tug at me from every direction. My body spins around, caught in the pull of the drain.

I shoot down an underground maze of pipes and tubing, and get belched out, dumped onto a cold, metal slab. I can't stop shivering. It's cold in here. Freezer burn bites at the tips of my fingers and toes.

My body gets pulled out of the freezer. I'm naked with nothing but a dingy modesty cloth splayed over my junk. A circle of morticians helmeted with respirator masks loom over me. They lather me up with disinfectant soap and a scrub brush. Give me a complete rubdown. The brush goes into every nook and cranny. Rasps too rough on my intimates. When they are done they bring out the high-pressure hose.

They let my body air dry before getting back to work. The morticians douse their gloves with baby oil and get ready. They slick my body with it: massage the back of my neck, flex the joints on my arms and legs, and give my neck a strong kneading to ease the stiffness. It feels sort of nice. My body responds and begins to slacken. The muscles relax. Turn into jelly.

That's when I notice them pulling out the syringes. This was all a trick. The bastards were just softening me up. Getting my meat good and tender for their needles.

I try to jump from the autopsy table, but my body remains motionless: it won't budge, my limbs keep slack, nothing responds, my nerve endings misfire, call out into a void, and fizzle out.

Two needles drive into my carotid arteries, a third one goes right into my jugular, and another set drills into the femoral veins near my groin. I get pumped full of the strong stuff, pure formaldehyde and methanol. The fumes give me a quick high. They waft up my nostrils and seep out through the hole in the back of my head.

The morticians let me marinate on the slab for a while. They bring out a pink makeup caboodle and a blow drier—puff up my hair to hide the bullet's exit wound, add blush, and a little gloss on my lips to give my skin the hint of life again. The undertakers snap a group picture with my body after they're finished; all grins, and thumbs-up at another job well done.

I get pushed back into the freezer, but I find myself slotted into an open coffin. My body's dressed in this cheap, gloomy looking suit that pinches at the pits. The pants are moth-eaten. A split runs down the back. It smells like bargain consignment shopping.

My body sweats in the afternoon heat. The temperature keeps rising and I'm already beginning to thaw. I can feel droplets of embalming fluid leak onto the suit. These stains aren't coming off anytime soon.

Mourners go by in a whirl above me. No time to notice any hint of the smell. They wait in line to see me like they just bought tickets. I watch them inspect my corpse, become mildly curious, get bored with it, and then go back to their own business.

I can smell the booze off their breaths. Spot the relief in their eyes.

They look tired of me already. My corpse isn't enough of a show. Their eyes wander. Faces downcast to fiddle with their phones. They all try to hide their smug, self-satisfied faces. Nobody's here to mourn me. They're pumped up. This is a victory lap. These fuckers think they are better than me just because they are still living and breathing. They lord this achievement over me like a heartbeat means something.

Lorraine passes by next. My girl wears a black, cowhide mini, and makes every man in the room stare longer than they should. She always knew how to dress to turn heads.

She stands over me for a while. The tattooed hearts up the stretch of her jugular bob as she swallows. She reaches into the coffin and stuffs a lock of her hair into my pocket.

Her miniskirt gives me a rise. She looks great. I want to call out to her, but I can't move. My tongue goes numb in my mouth. I feel tacked to this padded casket.

Lorraine grips the lid of the coffin and shuts me inside.

I feel the coffin getting lowered into the ground. Then the shoveling. The slap of dirt on the lid. The wood starts to creak as the earth piles on. It warps, flattening out as it gets compacted into the subsoil.

I start to panic, and buck against the lid, trying to crack it open. I kick at the hinges. Put my shoulder into it and keep ramming at it, but the thing won't budge. The lid must be wedged tight with overturned earth. I'm trapped.

The air down here thickens. I swallow it in mouthfuls. Desperate, I start feeling around in the dark, trying to find a weak spot in the coffin. I tear at the silk embroidery and padding. Rip it off in clumps until I get to the bare wood. My hands run over the smooth boards. Nails claw at the wood and peel off bloody shavings.

Nothing works. I gnash my teeth, bang my head against the lid, and rebound back on the padding. My skull is fucking killing me.

Something gleams in the far-end of the casket. I think it's just the concussion at first, but the thing won't stop glowing. The cold, metallic light pulses with a heartbeat. I reach into the darkness, and finger the casket's edges and exposed nail heads, until I find what I'm looking for: a lever.

I grip at the handle and pull. A red bulb flashes over my head. The coffin's alarm goes off. Suddenly, a trap door opens at my back, and I shoot down in a freefall.

I scream at the top of my lungs. My body drops in this kamikaze nosedive. I'm out of control, and picking up speed. My suit lights up with sparks. Patches of the cheap fabric burn as I enter into this new atmosphere. A gust of smoke trails behind me.

Everything slows as the ground closes in on me. All I can think of doing is covering my face. I take a deep breath, grit my teeth, and brace myself.

I crash-land on a pile of moving corpses. Bodies squirm all around me. They are everywhere. The corpses stack one on top of the other, a roiling monster of dead flesh. They crawl around four-legged, shoving and fighting and going wild, desperate to get out from the mass grave.

Severed limbs rain down as more bodies add to the pile. I try to avoid a huge motherfucker on his haunches, munching on an oversized, bleeding drumstick. Two old women roll around, fighting for space; they snap and bite at each other with their bare gums. I jump out of their way and bump into this girl pulling at the umbilical cord sticking from between her legs. Her skin feels slippery with sweat and blood. She grabs my lapels and begs for me to help her take the baby out. The woman puts my hand on her belly. The thing inside her gurgles and moves. I shake my head and run the other way.

It doesn't matter where I go. They keep on coming, more bodies falling from the sky. The stiffs drift around in a haze. They huddle together, shivering, sharing in each other's body heat. Some of them get on their knees and pray. Others run around, talking to themselves, lost in their own minds. The dead keep screaming, calling out strange names that mean nothing to me.

I break through the crowd and am about to get out, but one of the corpses manages to grab on to my leg. I look down at the thing holding me back. The freak is headless. It crawls around on all fours, growling and spitting juices from its neck stump. I kick at it until it lets off, and turn to go on my way, but the freak keeps following me. It growls and moves closer, getting more aggressive. The corpse circles around me. It sniffs my scent through its throat hole.

"I don't want any trouble," I try to calm it down.

But that thing has no sense in it anymore. Not since it lost its head. It just growls, and jumps me, knocking me back on my ass. The corpse pins me down with its knees, goes at me bare-knuckled, blind, and clumsy. It misses most of its punches, but still does some damage. My blood flecks over its bare chest.

I try to knock it off, but only manage to roll the corpse over. It's stuck on me like a tick. We keep wrestling, scuffing and rolling until we hit the bottom of the pile of bodies.

The corpse snarls, and swipes at me, scratch-marking my cheek. The cuts sting. My blood goes hot with anger. I make a fist, and punch it right on its throat hole. The corpse stumbles back with a gurgle, and runs off.

I wipe the blood from my face, and get back on my feet.

The world around me is something else. I try to take it all in. There's nothing but sand all around me. Glowing and radioactive. A desert wasteland.

The sky looks made out of solid stone. It looms over the horizon in the shape of a dome; its weight supported by mountain ranges, and columns of thick, volcanic minerals. Dead bodies slip from the dome's cracks and fall in a downpour, trailing sparks, screaming, and lighting up the sky.

An enormous fireball blazes above me. Flares spike out and torch the sky. The Planetary core. It heats up this world like an underground sun, a fallen star. Its light is blinding. I have to cover my eyes to avoid getting stung by its glare.

15

Sirens go off in the distance. Men in white uniforms and surgical masks roll in unmarked vans from the desert. They spread out in teams to drag the dead from the mass grave. Most of the corpses comply. They follow orders, and do as they are told; too stunned to do any different. The uniforms organize them into neat, never ending queues.

But not all of them are so easy to herd. A few of the stiffs try and make a break for it, and dash into the desert. The uniforms go after them. They take them down with tranquilizer guns and net launchers, hogtie them, and drag their bodies back to the unmarked shuttle vans cruising on the sand.

I sit back and look up at the sky, waiting for Lorraine to drop.

CHAPTER TWO

PARADISE COVE

Where are you? I'm waiting. Don't be afraid. It's so easy. All you got to do is drop.

She never shows.

I can't wait any longer. The last shuttle is out there flicking its highs beams and honking at me. I turn back at the sky one last time before running to the van.

The driver eyeballs me as I climb inside. He taps his watch. The van's already packed with dead bodies. All the seats look taken. A couple of girls lower the hems of their skirts as I pass to cover the lividity on their thighs. I hop over this kid coughing up something red on the aisle, and squeeze through the crowd of corpses hanging on to the van's overhead straps. They swing from side to side, pieces of meat on hooks. A group of old men in their hospital gowns take up the middle rows. They stay quiet and keep mostly to themselves, looking out the window, shaking their heads, legs spread and balls hanging.

An obese, jumbo looking corpse slumps over the back seat. He takes the whole bench but for a few inches. The guy's polite, though. He nods his head and scoots over. The corpse stuffs his intestines back through the slit on his belly, and wipes the seat clean for me. I squeeze between him and the window, close my eyes, and make them all disappear for the rest of the ride.

The shuttle's exhaust scrapes on the road. It rattles, and coughs out smoke the whole ride through. I breathe with my mouth, teeth gritted as a filter to avoid the stench wafting from the corpses all around me.

The van turns on a gravel road. It rounds a neat row of palm trees, and hits the breaks at the entrance of what looks like a dingy beach hotel. The van shrieks to a stop under a blinding, unreadable sign—markings long melted into blots of fiberglass and paint.

The driver hops off, opens the sliding door, and starts banging on the roof, hollering at us to get the hell out. Everybody is in a hurry. The corpses push and shove at each other to reach the exit. They pull at their hair, and tear their hospital gowns to shreds just to get ahead. A couple of the old buzzards go down and hit the floor with a scatter of teeth. They are all fucking animals looking out for themselves. Every man and woman here is on their own.

I wait in the back of the van until the stiffs settle down, and the aisle clears. I am the last one out. The driver taps his watch at me again.

I follow the others into the hotel lobby. A 'No Wi-Fi' sign hangs nailed over the doors. More men and women in those same white uniforms wait for us inside. Every one of them wears a surgical mask and latex gloves rolled up to their elbows. The staff looks crisp. They're overly starched and plastic looking. Their shorts and tennis skirts hug close to their thighs. Polo shirts are one size too small. They have great tans and bodies sculpted for beachwear. Pretty, but soulless characters that inhabit the worlds of beer commercials, highway billboards, and Spring Break movies.

My feet sink into the filthy carpeting. The pale, shitty shade of lima bean looks tracked with bloodstains. Green moss grows on the shag. Blind, slithering crawlers move through the fibers, and sniff at the feet of the guests.

A set of loud speakers play the same message in a constant loop, "Welcome to Paradise Cove, assisted afterlife facility, where the sun never sets. In case you're wondering, those are smiles behind our masks!"

I'm approached by a member of the staff. Another girl cloned with the same sun-licked beach body. Yellow hair just like Lorraine's. She waves at me even though she's right in front of me. The nametag tacked on her chest is completely blank.

"Welcome to Paradise Cove," she says. "We're super excited to meet you. I'm Ginny, one of your activities coordinators."

She puts a wreath of white lilies over my neck, hands me a plastic bag full of towels, and a gift basket. I sift through the goodies to see if anything catches my eye. It's stocked with a can of bug repellent, a six-pack of formaldehyde, and a gallon vat of tanning lotion.

She hands me my key card. I reach for it while trying to juggle the basket, and the bag of towels, and accidentally graze against her. We touch only slightly, not enough for me to even notice; but Ginny does. She stiffens at the contact. Her eyes pop from their sockets. She steps back. Ginny squirts hand sanitizer into her palms.

"Please don't touch the staff." She points to a sign on the wall. "We don't know where you dead things have been."

"Sorry," I want to wipe my hands on my pants like they're covered in something deadly.

"No problemo," she says, playing cheery again, "Follow me to your bungalow."

Ginny doesn't stop eyeballing me. She reminds me to keep my distance. The girl gets all sorts of out of shape if I get too close. She lifts her skirt to show me the gun tucked into her garters. Says she isn't afraid to use it. I walk a couple of paces behind her, trying to give her plenty of space.

I follow her down the hall. That yellow hair of hers bounces off her shoulders. The color triggers something inside me. Ginny starts to change. I start seeing things—Lorraine reflected back to me. Red hearts sprout on her neck. The eyes warp with an angry slant, turning hard and familiar. The groove of her crooked smile flashes just for me. I want to bury myself into her arms, hold her tight, and never let go. All I want is one whiff of that yellow hair.

But I hold myself back. It's not really her. This is all in my fucked up head. I rub my hands over my face to pull myself together. Shake off the hallucinations. I decide to make the best out of this situation and try to make out the outline of Ginny's panties. Enjoy the bounce of her ass under the prim, white skirt.

Ginny gives me a tour of the hotel. The poor girl seems bored and going through the motions, having done this same routine for an eternity already. She takes me to the gift shop and the cafeteria. Shows me around the gym. Ginny wipes the dust from the machines. She opens the doors to the steam room. Says it is out of order.

We stop at the hotel bar next, but we can't get inside. It is already packed to capacity. I try to take in the vibe of the crowd. All I get is the feel of a depressing watering hole. Nobody seems to be having a good time. The stiffs drink heavy. They stare at the television screens and keep to themselves. The waitresses look pretty, though. They all carry fresh rounds of the same glowing, pink cocktail.

I spot a couple of vending machines out in the corridor, so I close in to have a look. The dispensers are stocked with live baby moles. The animals squirm inside plastic wrappers. The little guys press their pink noses on the bags and fog up the plastic. The moles on the bottom racks have wasted to nothing but skeletons. The tags on the bags read, 'Best purchased before they die.'

Ginny snaps her fingers at me. She reminds me she's on a schedule, "You should be excited. We got you placed in an oceanfront bungalow."

I turn away from the baby moles and follow her outside.

I step out of the hotel onto a golden beach. I try to trace the crescent shaped coastline with my eyes, but it stretches out into the horizon and seems to go on without an end. The planetary core heats up the ocean, and brings it to a boil. The water smokes as the waves lap against the sprawling bay.

The hotel's guests lie on their backs, baking in the heat, getting fried by the radioactive burn of the planetary core. Flies stick to their backs. They look like big, lounging lizards. Their skin toasted, hardened into scales. The stiffs take off their sunglasses; they stretch out and yawn—reptiles reanimated by the surge of heat in their blood.

I walk by the beach and watch the corpses float face down on the water. I can't knock this feeling that I'm being followed. Something buzzes on the nape of my neck. Smoke gathers in a cloud behind me. Its tendrils sneak up and squeeze my throat, taking the shape of black, alien fingers. I turn around to face whatever is at my back, but the cloud disperses, and blows off with the wind—there's nothing there.

I eyeball the stiffs on the beach and notice that there's an old man staring at me. He sits perched on top of the lifeguard tower, a pair of binoculars trained right smack in my direction. A cold, burning light glints off from the lenses. The old man has me in his sights. Death hides just behind his eyes.

He wears an expensive looking white suit—linen, something that breathes in this heat. The sleeves roll up to his forearms. The collar is spiked. A tilted panama hat blackens half of his face with shade. The old man takes a drag from his cigarette. The smoke puffs into a cloud at his back and spirals into a pair of black wings. They splay out and cast an inky shadow across the beach.

My bungalow is still a bit far off. Ginny shows me up the steps to a small beachfront terrace. I struggle to slip the key card into the door, while holding on to the gift basket, and the fucking towels. Ginny is, of course, of no help.

I work the key and kick the door open. It's pretty cramped inside. Barely enough room for me. There's no bed. No bathroom. Only a swivel chair, a dresser and a TV set. The television is already on. The same thing plays on every channel: footage of some sort of race. The players climb up the impossible cliffs and mountains outside. They make their way up the rock, getting higher and higher into the sky; nothing but dots on the horizon.

I circle around the room, an animal testing the limits of his cage, "It's sort of been a long trip. Where's the bathroom?"

"You're dead. It doesn't work that way anymore. We offer a complementary disembowelment procedure once your intestinal tract fills up. Welcome to Paradise Cove." Ginny hurries out of the room.

I find the closet and dump the towels and gift basket inside. The swivel chair looks uncomfortable, but there's nowhere else to rest. I cradle myself into the seat, knees pressed against my chest. My eyes close, and I try to sleep.

But something's wrong. Light creeps in from the windows. The television set buzzes in the background. Nothing clicks into place. Sleep doesn't come. My eyes spring back open.

I spin around in that chair for hours. The sun won't budge. The thing never sets. It is getting annoying. The heat feels unbearable. I reach into my pocket and finger the lock of Lorraine's hair.

I got nothing but you in my mind. Where are you? You always said I couldn't make it without you.

I can't get her out of my head. Her touch. The feel of her breath on my skin. Those heart-shaped tattoos that climb the vein on her throat. The whites of her eyes when she rolled them back at me.

But she's gone. A reverb in my head. Nothing but a ghost. Lorraine's not coming back for me. I'm all alone.

I go back into the closet, empty the towels from the plastic bag, and untie the ribbon on top of the gift basket. My head works on instinct. I improvise as I go. I put the bag over my head and fasten it shut with the ribbon.

The plastic clings to me as I breathe. The suction makes it stick to the hole in the back of my head. The bag fogs up. The air goes thick. I get dizzy with carbon monoxide and start to feel faint. It's working, dying all over again. Round two.

I smile wide, and tongue the plastic—this is why they call it an exit bag.

CHAPTER THREE

LEROY

All I do is sit there with the bag sucked on my face. My heart doesn't beat. It just lies there. Playing dead. Not one lousy pump. Something is off with me. I'm not feeling this suicide.

The doorknob shakes from side to side. I look up, startled. A plastic card slides through the crack in the frame. It screws around with the latch, prodding against the metal bolt until the spring mechanism gives, and the door swings open.

Someone walks into the room. The guy's a blur behind the plastic bag. He's tall. Lanky. Black, I think. He wears shades and an ankle-length overcoat.

The guy moves with a slinky feline cool, feeling around in the darkness with a cane roped around his wrist. He goes straight for the closet and starts stuffing my towels inside his coat.

"What are you doing?" I ask him.

He doesn't answer. Let's my question hang in the air. Some dark cloud roils in my belly. My blood goes up. I never could take being ignored.

"I said, what the fuck do you think you're doing?" I ask harder this time.

"Go about your business," he says. "There is nothing to worry about. My name is Leroy. I'm blind. It's all official. Sealed and notarized. You can trust me."

"Are you stealing my towels?"

He turns to me like he can see me, "You want me to spell it out for you? I'm ripping you off."

"Get the fuck out of my bungalow!" I play up manliness from under the bag. "Can't you see I'm busy here?"

I regret my words just as they come out. Now it's my turn to stay quiet. My tongue always gets me into trouble.

"You got a big mouth on you, don't you?" He thwacks his cane hard against his palm, "Name yourself?"

"Bloom," I answer.

"Let me school you about the ways of the world, Bloom. When a blind man rips you off just lie there and take it. That's just common sense. Fucking manners. Good Karma."

"Sorry..."

"You should be. Do you know how hard these are to come by? This is currency, baby. I've been waiting over five years for a new towel. Front desk doesn't give a shit. You noobs got it so easy, everything is handed to you, and you don't even know it."

"Fine take them. I don't need them anymore, anyway." My voice sounds muffled by the plastic crackling over my mouth.

"I can hear you wheezing through that plastic bag." Leroy pulls it off my face. "You're not trying to kill yourself, are you? That would be a very bad idea. You don't want to do that here. Believe me, death is a spiral, the deeper you go the worse it gets."

"I've been trying to off myself for hours but nothing happens."

"Dying's tougher the second time around. Our bodies start building a resistance to it."

I scratch the hole in the back of my head, "Never a break…"

"You sound like a moper. Don't tell me this is all about pussy?" Leroy asks.

"Well, sure, my girl, Lorraine," I admit.

"Face it. You're dead. You aren't getting laid again. Unless, you stick with me." He nudges my ribs with his cane.

I let Leroy charm me without putting up much of a fight; he takes every single one of my towels before he leaves.

CHAPTER FOUR

ZOMBIE

I go for a walk to get my mind off everything. Screams echo through the ventilation shafts and haunt after me. My head spins. I feel fevered. Eyeballs pickled and salted. I am on no sleep.

The air conditioners gurgle and piss sludge on the carpet. All they do is rile the heat. Every stiff walking by sweats out a soup of formaldehyde and methanol. I wipe the goop from my face, smell it on my fingers, and almost retch from the stink.

I stumble around in a haze, hunched over and dragging my feet, playing the zombie. The guests look at me like I'm crazy. They whisper to each other. Shake their heads. Hold on to their beach towels. Look the other way as I pass them by.

All they see is a freak show. But that isn't new. It was just the same when I was living. There has always been something wrong with me. I never was any good at being human. I felt different. Marked. People seemed so alien to me. I could never make meaningful connections to anyone other than Lorraine. She was my only touchstone to that world.

I never fit in back there. All I ever did when I had a heartbeat was run away from my life, drinking and doping myself to escape out of it, never manning up to the moment, until that one day when I finally found my nerve, and blew out the back of my head.

Down here, it's just the same. It all seems fucking magnified for some reason. I am not like the rest of the guests here at Paradise Cove. I am not one of them. I can't be. No way. I am not just another corpse.

Fluorescent lights flicker as I walk past. I turn the corner at the end of the hall, and come up to a group of school girls hanging around the vending machines. The girls wear skintight uniforms, and share the same matching wrist slits. They giggle to each other, peering at the baby moles in the machines. The animals wheeze for breath inside their individually packaged plastic baggies.

I push the girls aside and tap at the glass. The moles stare at me from inside the machine. Their pupils dilate and almost cover the entire eyeball. They show nothing but fear. I feel for the fuckers. They're trapped underground just like me. I put my shoulder into it, and ram against the glass, but I bounce off and land on my ass.

I start to draw a crowd. The guest's gather around me and snicker. I keep going at it again and again. Kicking and bashing at the display window. But the thing won't even crack. I squeeze my arms through the drawer at the base of the machine and reach for the moles, but I can't get to the little guys.

A woman stands by a nearby doorway and chuckles at me, "You're not the first one to try and save those poor suckers. But trust me, you won't. No one can. They're already doomed."

I look her over. She has an ugly face, but an okay body. Her hips are wide and her thighs have plenty of meat on them. But she's hit middle age and her curves have already started to warp into a sag.

"Down here long?" she asks.

"I'm a noob."

She licks her lips, and leans back on the door frame, "This is your lucky night. I'll give you the best fuck of your afterlife for the price of a hand towel. What do you say, nooby?"

"I'm fresh out. I just got ripped off."

She smiles, "I'm a sucker for fresh corpses. Nothing beats rigor mortis. How about a freebie?"

I think it over. The offer makes my blood rise and my cock go bone hard. I can't help it. I haven't gotten laid in a while. The dead hooker's nothing special to look at, but I decide to go with it: have a quick fuck and bust a load. All I got to do is avoid looking at her straight in the face. I promise myself to think of Lorraine.

The hooker pulls me into her bedroom. She spits into her hand and slips it inside my pants. Her grip is cold, but the woman knows how to work it. She rolls back the foreskin and strokes at the head. I paw at her hips and moan.

"I haven't done this since I died," I mutter.

"Don't worry," she winks. "I got more holes than you'll ever need."

She drops her dress. Her body looks riddled with budding, purple bullet holes. The wounds pucker up like gnarled mouths. Her tits are shot to pieces. The flesh blackened with gunpowder burns. Nipples blown off. I can see right through her. There is a big, gaping crater right where her heart should be.

I get the hell out of the room.

CHAPTER FIVE

SIGNS OF EARLY RIGOR MORTIS

I explore the other side of the hotel and stumble into a spa. The idea sounds inviting after that whole hooker mess. I want to get clean, relax, and let the stress slurp off my bones. Forget everything I've seen since I got here. I decide to indulge myself. Something I've always been good at. I am no stranger to giving myself away to pleasure.

One of the attendants smokes a cigarette outside the entrance. He's another interchangeable hard body. His muscles pop from underneath his polo shirt without even trying. Flexing is as natural as breathing for him.

He rolls his eyes, and puts on a surgical mask as I approach, "Can I help you?"

I try to read his nametag but the thing is blank, "I need to relax."

"Just look at yourself." He inspects the back of my head. "You're already coming apart."

"Leave me alone, I'm dead."

He introduces himself. Says his name is Shane. I do not believe him.

I ask him why he doesn't write his name on the tag, "Isn't that why it's there for?"

Shane doesn't answer me. His face turns expressionless. Stone. He's annoyed, but doesn't show it. A good trick, something he's practiced and clearly mastered.

I'm impressed. That is a skill I never learned. Always did have a quick triggered temper. Short fucking fuse. Some dark cloud storming inside of me. A demon in the blood. What can I say? I'm an emotional guy.

There are things inside all of us that we cannot control. Monsters beneath the skin. We bare them, and live with the guilt.

Shane tells me to follow him, but warns me not to get too close.

I follow him into the spa and take a look around the place. Steam rises from the baths of hot wax and paraffin. Dead women bake under heating lamps. Their skin looks golden, tans smooth and spotless. The stiffs get dolled up—flipping the pages of dead celeb glossies, scheduling manicures for nails that never stop growing, polishing their grisly skeleton faces.

Shane sits me down on a chair, covers my eyes with a pair of cucumber pads, and dips my feet in a vat of mud that squishes between my toes.

"I'll give it to you straight," he says. "You've got a hell of a mess back there. You're already going soft. The back of your skull is about to collapse. You're going to need the full works: a complete plastination rejuvenation. But don't worry, all we got to do is dehydrate your body, impregnate you with liquid plastic, and let your body harden. I'll have you out of here in no time."

"Impregnate?" I ask

He feels around the wound in the back of my head, "Plastination preserves what's left of your body. It makes it last a little longer. You'll feel like new again; a young corpse with signs of early rigor mortis."

Shane takes me to the acetone tanks. He slips a finger into the liquid and says the temperature is just right. I dip into one of the tanks. The liquid feels freezing. I can't stop shaking. Swallowing acetone in mouthfuls. The chemical stings down my throat. But I grit my teeth and manage to bear it. I marinate in the freezing goop for a while, watching it fizz and carbonate, and dry my body out.

He pokes at my skin, until the texture feels right to him. I hop out from the tank and let him continue his inspection. He lifts my feet to check between my toes, fingers my pits, and taps on my belly.

He asks me to climb up on a gurney. I get on it and stare at the ceiling. A black, fungal growth covers everything but the fluorescent lamps. Flies stick to the bulbs, drawn in by the light.

Shane rolls the plastination machine to my bedside. The tentacles swing as it comes closer. The machine is a just a motorized pump attached to a rolling stove. The stove gurgles with a vat of liquid plastic that boils on its burners. Eight hoses stick out from the bubbling soup.

He screws a needle to the end of each hose, "This is going to hurt."

Shane stabs the needles at the pits of my arms and legs, rams a pair into my ribcage, and three more around my navel, one painful bastard goes right through my eyeball. He works at the foot pedal and gets the motor started. Sizzling plastic squirts under my skin. The liquid pumps into my body. It burns as it spreads. Cooks me from the inside. The pain is fucking unbearable.

I scream, "Stop!"

He rolls his eyes, "What is it?"

"I can't take it anymore. This is fucking horrible. Isn't there another way of keeping off the rot other than cooking me in plastic?"

He shrugs his shoulders, "You can go lie in a shallow pit in the beach and let the planetary core dry the leather on your corpse."

I unplug the needle from my eyeball, "I'll take my chances out there."

CHAPTER SIX

CHECKING OUT

I burst into the lobby. The place looks jam-packed. Fresh arrivals keep on coming. There is no shortage of corpses in this place. I spot a crowd of tourists fished out from some plane accident. Their remains are scattered into pieces over this transparent, plastic tarp. The staff tag the loose body parts and sort them into piles. A queue to reclaim their missing bits runs in a circle around the room, and goes out into the parking lot. The tourists drag themselves on their hands and knees, smearing rings of blood on the carpet.

I push through the tourists and work my way to the front desk.

The receptionist looks up at me with a discrete eye roll, "Welcome to Paradise Cove. In case you're wondering there is a smile behind my mask."

"I want to check out."

She cocks her head, "Why would you want to do a thing like that?

"Does it matter? I just want to leave."

"That makes no sense. You are making no sense, sir."

"Why is that?"

"The sun never sets here. Haven't you read the brochures? You are in a paradise."

"If you really want to know, this place you got here is a living fucking hell. I want to check out, now!" I bang my fist on the counter.

"No, no, no, you got this all wrong. There is no such thing as checking out." She squints at her computer's screen. "What is your room number? Name Yourself?"

"There has to be some mistake…"

"No mistake," she says.

I close in on her face and she recoils, "Now listen to me very carefully. This is your last shot. You're not getting another. Nod if you understand."

She does.

"You are getting me the fuck out of this place!"

I'm getting loud and heads start to turn. Shuttle drivers and other hotel staff collect by the door way. They eyeball me, and nod to each other in my direction. My big mouth always gets me into trouble. Never did learn how to keep it shut.

I try to sound calm, but don't manage the trick; my voice stays thick with anger, "Listen to me, I just want to go back home."

The receptionist rolls her eyes, "Don't we all, honey. Next!"

CHAPTER SEVEN

DEATH HAS NO PAYOFF

Where are you? I'm still waiting. Did you forget about me? We had a date, remember? You and I were supposed to spend eternity together. Everybody said it. We were perfect for each other. We were both doomed.

I pull up a tanning chair and laze about on the beach. The planetary core orbits above me. Its heat feels good—slurps off the stress, takes the stiffness out of my muscles, and reanimates my cold body. I slip out of my jacket and unbutton my dress shirt. I tie it around my forehead like a turban to soak up the sweat. My toes dig into the irradiated sand.

Who knows how long I've been down here. I can't tell time anymore. The sun never sets. It doesn't section the day off into pieces. There are no neat little packages down here. Everything turns into a blur; one moment jumbles, and crashed lands into another. The feeling becomes overwhelming. After a while it all starts to feel like an endless sweep of moments that just keep on coming, no breaks, lulls, or breathers.

I dig into my pocket and curl my fingers into the lock of Lorraine's hair. We have never been apart for this long. It feels strange that I can exist without her. We have such a long history together. We have been an item since we were kids. Lorraine and I know nothing else but each other.

This all seems like a fucking waste. Nothing ever really changes for me. I can't escape the gnawing feeling that I'm out of place. That I don't belong here. I hated my life when I was up there. Now I'm miserable down here. Nothing, no place, ever seems to satisfy.

Things never quite worked out for me up there. I was never able to get anything going when I was living. I went through a parade of shit jobs, repeating the same cycle, over and over again: going from paid training to entry level positions, bouncing out of there before the probation periods were done. I was a lost cause. Lorraine and I might have shared an apartment, but it was her money that paid for it. We lived our lives on her dime. It was all hers.

I didn't come from a bad place. Things just went wrong for me somewhere. I got lost or something. Went down the wrong motherfucking road. I feel like I've been dealt a bad hand—another sucker that's just been grifted. I was a fool to believe it. Death has no pay off.

I spot a waiter and whistle at him to get his attention. He hesitates, takes his time about it, but eventually comes over. I ask him for a drink, the coldest thing in the back of his freezer. He takes my order holding the tray in front of him like a shield, afraid to get too close to me.

A warm breeze tunnels through my head wound. The insides of my skull prickle. I try to close my eyes and veg out in the sun, but these volleyball players on the beach are making too much of a racket. Every one of them looks gym rat big. Pretty much rock-cut. Their muscles pop from under a thick crust of charcoal that covers their entire bodies. They have all been burned to a black crisp. The boys hoot when one of them spikes the ball— they high five each other, make out hard, and paw at their asses. Some of them are still smoking, ashes flaking on the sand.

The woman sitting in the tanning chair next to mine clicks her tongue at them. Her toes curl lewdly. She sunbathes topless. Her y-incision looks like a rush job. It runs in a zigzag from her collar right through the gap in between her tits, and bends at angle toward her belly button.

I smile at her, scooting my chair closer to hers. She lowers her sunglasses and rolls her eyes at me. I scoot right back where I started.

The waiter comes back with my order. He brings over one of those hot pink cocktails I've seen all over this place. The drink flickers with a radioactive glow. The waiter's shaking only gets worse as he comes closer to me. The kid goes into a fit. He can barely hold on to the tray. The poor guy's scared shitless. He digs the base of the glass into the sand, and runs away.

The staff here at Paradise Cove are all the same. They think the guests are medieval lepers. The fuckers fear us like something diseased, possibly contagious. And maybe they are right. You never know. I can't help but feel a little dirty. I am a dead thing. My body rotted in the ground. I can try and ignore the smell, but that does not mean it's not there.

I swirl the pink drink in my mouth. It's not so bad, sort of sweet with an aftertaste of grenadine and anise. The drink is strong. It has a hell of a kick to it. I work up a buzz pretty quickly. The sugary deliciousness is addictive. I gulp it down and sink into the tanning chair as it burns inside my belly.

I look around the beach, and spot Leroy over by the dolphin tank. He slinks about, quick and stealthy, pinching the volleyball player's towels.

I run up to him, actually excited to see him, "Need more currency?"

"Hey…" he feels my face, "it's the mopey motherfucker. How're you doing, Bloom? Still on suicide watch?"

"Don't worry about it. That's nothing new. I'm always depressed," I mutter.

"Well there's no helping that, you're dead," he says. "Still down about your girl?"

"I guess so."

The dolphins play around and chase each other inside the tank. I tap at the glass and the animals get startled by the noise. They pop out from the water and stare at me with their wet, oily eyes.

"So this girl of yours. What happened?" Leroy asks.

I tell him everything, "Her name is Lorraine. She's a lost soul, just like me. Lorraine and I didn't belong up there. We never fit. We saw that world of the living for what it really was: a waiting room for the graveyard, just another dark corner to die in. There was no point in staying there. It only delayed the inevitable. We wanted to get it over with. Cut the bullshit. End it on our own terms. We planned on finding a little love nest on the other side. Promised to keep it all to ourselves.

"We were going for a suicide pact sort of thing; making a real commitment. It was going to be very romantic. I bought candles. She drew a warm bubble bath. We went all out. I died first, ate the gun, and pulled the trigger. Lorraine, well, she didn't follow."

He shakes his head, "Damn…that's cold. She left you hanging?"

I shrug my shoulders. "I don't know."

The dolphins don't stop staring at me. They squint their oily eyes into slits. Bubbles rise in the water. I reach into the tank to pet them, but the animals back up into a corner with their needle teeth bared.

I pull my hand back, "I don't think they like me."

"Don't bother the dolphins," Leroy says, "Dead things spook them."

Leroy maneuvers past the stiffs tanning on the beach without a need for eyes. He senses the world with nothing but his cane. It sticks out like the tongue of a snake and draws undulating lines in the sand.

I feel someone breathing down my neck. His breath is hot on my skin. I can feel it blowing against the bullet wound in the back of my head. He feels right on top of me. I turn around, and spot the old man again.

The old man on top of the lifeguard tower glares at me through his binoculars. A mop of white hair ripples with the wind under his Panama hat. He points right at me, letting me know that he means business. His eyes are on me, and always watching.

I turn to Leroy, "Who is that old man in the lifeguard tower?"

He stiffens; pushes his shades up the bridge of his nose, "Act natural. Pretend you don't see it. Whatever you do, never look it in the eye."

I'm tempted to look over my shoulder. Almost do, but Leroy turns me back.

His voice lowers, "It's a reaper. You don't want to get that thing riled. That old man is the enforcer down here. It keeps the dead in line."

I try to ignore him, pretend he's not there, watching me. But I can't help it; I've always been bad at resisting temptation. I sin

40

easy. The old man draws me to him. I peek at him from the corner of my eyes, and get caught by his gaze. He lowers the binoculars and stares at me with his bare eyes—a pair of blinding, icy orbs that cook my retinas with a cold burn.

"So what are you going to do about it, Bloom?" Leroy asks.

I rub the sting from my eyeballs, "About what?"

"Lorraine. Your girl."

"She's up there and I'm down here. There is nothing I can do."

"I don't know about that…" Leroy thinks out loud.

"If I could just talk to her again everything would be alright." I grip the lock of her hair in my pocket. "I'm sure she would drop everything, and kill herself on the spot. She would come down here to join me just like we planned."

"I don't get it? Why would you want to bring someone you love to a place like this?"

"To be together," I say, simply.

Leroy shakes his head, "You're a weak sister, aren't you? First things first. You got to man up and confront her. You have to find out why she didn't come after you. Trust me. If you don't, this will eat at you for an eternity."

"I can't say I am not curious."

"There are ways to commune with the living," he says, "if you have the money for it. You're gonna need more towels."

CHAPTER EIGHT

GRAVE ROBBER

I hide behind a palm tree and watch them. The guests laze about on a row of tanning chairs neatly aligned by the shore. Flies hover over their bodies. The stiffs sip on their pink cocktails and work on their tans. Their skin looks toasted, cracked into lozenge shaped scales. They roil in the heat, breathing heavy, and enjoy the spike of temperature in their blood.

I get down on all fours and start crawling. My chest grazes on the sand. I dart from a batch of palm trees and hide behind the legs of a barbeque grill, then make a dash past the bonfires billowing smoke on the coastline. I keep creeping closer and closer to them.

Nobody notices me. The guests space out—stare blankly at the ocean licking at the beach. I see no life in them. Vital signs are low. Their breathing sounds fake and affected. They smell like death. Nothing close to human anymore.

They are easy pickings. The suckers almost take it willingly. They sit there asking for it. I sneak up behind them and steal as many towels as I can get my hands on.

I scurry away and hide behind the palm trees to check out my loot. I've managed to gather a big pile already. The towels feel soft bundled in my lap, but they spark at me with static. They shoot electricity through my fingers, and rouse my nerve endings. A high rushes through me. For a second there I almost feel a heartbeat again.

The electric high only keeps on building. It riles me up inside. My shoulders hunch and my head hangs low—teeth bared like a predator's. I prowl around the beach in search of another mark. Skulking around in the sand, stealing from the dead, it gives me the feel of a desert grave robber.

I spot a perfect mark by the surf. A kid all on his own, building sandcastles by the water. The little guy has the look leukemia on him. He's bald and wafer thin. Catheter track marks go up his arms and legs. Easy pickings.

He wears an oversized beach towel as a cape. A big, yellow smiley face is stamped on the back. The kid scoops out wet sand from a bucket and lays the mortar for a new turret to protect his keep. This hell is a sweet vacation for him. Poor little sucker, he doesn't see me coming.

I sneak up behind him and try to yank the towel from his back, but the kid holds on to the other end. We tug and pull, and struggle for a while. The kid is a tenacious bastard. He won't give in and is stronger than he looks. There is a mean streak to him. He throws a handful of sand into my eyes.

My blood goes up. Black smoke rises. The demon comes out again. I just react. I gnash my teeth, sucker punch the little bastard to the ground, and make a run for it.

The kid starts crying. Squealing, really. He belts those suckers out. The little bastard throws himself on the ground, kicking and screaming, throwing a shit storm of a tantrum.

He starts to draw a crowd. The stiffs get up from their tanning chairs, and come out from the ocean for him. A large mob circles around the little shit. Women coo all over him and stroke his bald head. The kid knows how to milk the attention. He keeps asking for his smiley face towel and his mommy.

I don't trust the kid. He's shifty; has violence in his eyes. Unforgiving. The bastard has the look of a squealer. This could get ugly. I try to mix in with the other guests walking on the beach, and get as far away from the mob as possible. But I can't help looking back. Curiosity always does it for me.

This mean-looking meathead with an axe buried into the side of his skull takes the kid on his lap and asks him who did this to him. The little shit wipes his crocodile tears and points right at me.

The mob surges, and I start running. They pelt at me with anything they can get their hands on—rocks, empty bottles, and cocktail glasses. A tanning a chair flies over my head. Broken glass scatters everywhere. I get hit in the shins. Smacked by a rock in the jaw. The shelling doesn't stop.

This is getting hairy. I pick up my pace—dodge and weave past the stiffs, and jump over a row of tanning chairs arranged on the beach. I knock a couple of the waiters out of my way and send their trays crashing.

The meathead with the axe buried into his head closes in on me. His shirt is off and the guy looks hardened. Black hairs bristle from his shoulders down to his spine. He's all snorts and grunts. A cloud of sand rises at his back. He dislodges the axe head from his skull and hurls the blade at me.

The blade whizzes over my head. It spins like a propeller and stabs into the trunk of a palm tree. I almost piss myself. My knees go weak. That was a close one. Fucking lucky break. I grin at the meathead, and flip him off before gunning it back to the dolphin tank.

I manage to lose the mob and make my way back to the dolphins. The animals surface from the water to eyeball me again. They bare their teeth and hiss, spitting at me from their blowholes.

Leroy paces around under a palm tree lit up like a Christmas tree. I catch my breath and run up to him with my cache of towels. He feels them over like he's impressed.

"Ok. You learn fast. Not bad for your first run."

I feel winded and almost double over, "Thank you, Leroy."

"That was a sweet move stealing that kid's towel, by the way. Cold. Show no mercy. Take no prisoners. Only way to go."

"Do I have enough towels to pay her fee yet?" I ask.

"The Sybil is a big woman," he answers, "a whole lot of flesh to dry."

"Is she any good?"

"You noobs have no idea what's going on, do you? The Sybil's only the best bio-spiritualist in all the nine charted hells. That woman can summon the spirits of the living and suck them down to the realm of the dead. She picks their souls like flies."

I try to flag down the waiters for a drink, but every single one of them is hell bent on ignoring me.

"This hotel sucks," I shake my head. "What are we supposed to be doing here anyway? Turning extra-crispy under the sun?"

"We're waiting," Leroy says.

"For what?"

"Nobody knows. But we got all the time in the world for it."

Chapter Nine

The Dig

Can you feel it? I am coming for you. There's no fighting it. We'll be together soon.

Leroy counts his paces. He moves through this place blind as a bat, using memory triggers to help him map his surroundings. All he needs is something familiar, a little orientation, and his autopilot sets in. He picks up his pace to a sprint. The tip of his cane feels out the surface of the beach. He is on to something buried underneath. Its magnetic pull draws him closer and closer.

He kneels under a diseased, bald palm tree, rolls up his sleeves, and starts digging. Leroy finds what he's looking for a few feet under the sand—a large cement lid hidden in the ground. He pulls at a roll of chain attached to the manhole cover with a grunt. The lid looks heavy. It takes him a couple of tries to dislodge it, and uncover the entrance to a winding, black spider hole.

"This way," Leroy says.

I look down the spider hole, but can't see bottom. The passage goes on for miles, narrowing, getting inkier. It swallows every bit of light. I stick my arm inside and watch it disappear. The darkness lures me closer to the edge.

Leroy snaps his fingers at me. My face reflects in his shades. He tilts his head, points towards the mouth of the spider hole, and then shoots down the shaft. I follow.

My ankles give in when I hit bottom; I topple over and land on my back. It takes me a while to get adjusted to the dark. It's a total blackout down here. The ground feels uneven, cobblestoned with ragged slabs of rock. I stagger around, clumsy and stumbling, clawing the walls to keep myself upright.

Leroy moves around easily in the dark. He glides like a shadow cast on the walls. He knows every step, has memorized every turn, and plotted out this underground grid in his mind. Darkness does not faze him. He thrives in it—a burrowing animal in his own element.

A maze of underground tunnels, open mouthed caves, and warrens spread out in every direction. The walls are pockmarked with holes burrowed by pencil-thin worms that slip through, and wriggle on the ground.

I run my fingers on a web of pirate electrical wiring coiled on the ceiling, "What is this place?"

"The Catacombs," Leroy says, "Another world for those of us that don't care for the one that others made for us."

Dirt sprinkles on me from above. I look up at the ceiling again and notice it's riddled with cracks. "This place looks like it gonna cave in on us."

"Cave-ins happen every day," Leroy fixes his shades, matter of fact about it, "Be careful, you don't want to spend your afterlife crushed under a mountain of dirt without a coffin. A man needs his privacy. And there's a whole manner of critters alive and squirming down here... Worms are the wiliest. Single minded, bastards. Those fucker's will blow your asshole to the size of a grapefruit, if you're not careful."

I follow him down one of the tunnels. It leads to a large steel door hinged against the rock. A slot opens at the bottom of the metal frame. One hand sticks out: the digits move stiffly, nibs turned purple with frost-bite, thumbs and pinkies long gone. Leroy stuffs a wad of towels through the slot, and the door creaks open.

Leroy turns to me and asks, "Are you ready to see her again?"

I swallow hard, nod at him, and step inside.

The place looks jam-packed. Dead things stumble around drunk and hooting, knocking back shots with a vengeance. The corpses catcall at the waitresses, tapping their asses, sticking their fingers under their skirts, getting a feel of cold panties. They're loud. Sloppy. Break bottles over each other's heads. Get into knife fights. Dance on the tables. Snort live fire ants. Dry hump in the dark corners of the cave. The corpses are out of control. Nothing to hide, nothing to lose, and nothing to look forward to.

I have to walk sideways to squeeze through the crowd. It stinks thick to something sweet in here, a hint of chemicals and rot—corpse sweat. There are no ventilation shafts. No extractor fans. Nothing but tacky mouthfuls of carbon monoxide. But it's no problem, really. Breathing's not a big deal for the dead.

All eyes fix on the stage. Everybody turns to watch the three dead strippers sliding down a set of aluminum poles. The girls have moves. They slide upside down, their backs arched, tits out, legs expertly hooked on the steel. The strippers land in a handstand. They do an inverted split, and spread eagle for the crowd.

The girls get back on their feet, and start removing their loose body parts, popping their arms and legs right out of their sockets, trying out each other's gams on for size, testing the better fit— giving the crowd what it likes.

"Where am I…?" I mutter.

"Nowhere. If anybody asks, you were never here," Leroy says. "The demons upstairs are on to us. This place is an oasis in their wasteland. They want to destroy it. The hotel staff dynamites and seals shut every tunnel that they can find."

I follow him through the crowd. Waitresses move around us holding up these hexagonal trays made out of the lids of kiddie coffins. They serve roasted snakes straight on the skillet, skinned and barbequed. The stiffs gorge themselves on honey beetles and caramelized ants. They suckle on the big assed, crunchy queens. Curl centipedes with their forks like spaghetti. Crack open turtle shells for the meat inside. Munch on screeching, live beetles. This place specializes on serving low borne crawlers, burrowing insects, things that slither from their holes. The laminated menus read, "Eat them, before they eat you!"

We head to the bar to find a couple of empty seats. A group of sailors slam their bath towels on the counter. They're placing bets with the bookie behind the register. The guys lean drunkenly on each other, hair wet, skin bloated, covered with a thick, fungal slime. The sailors burp out saltwater.

One of the stiffs drinking at the counter jumps from his stool and joins the sailors. He pats them on their lower back, pretty close to their asses. The guy can't help it. He's a few inches short of a dwarf; a tiny little thing on stubby legs. His upper body overcompensates for his overall size and bubbles up with muscle.

The little guy walks with a wobble. A shaggy hide that looks flayed off the back of a yeti drags behind him. He introduces himself to the sailors. Says his name is Tulbahadur, the best jockey in the whole damned resort. He tells the sailors to bet on him in the races if they want a sure thing.

I try to swoop in and get to a couple of stools that just opened up, but the crowd gets rowdy with the action on the TV, and I get shoved back—bumping into the jockey, and making the little guy spill his drink all over his face. Tulbahadur turns to me. His face drips with cheap booze. The little guy drops his furs, juts out his bare chest, and pushes me back. He gets all aggressive, going off in a rant in his native tongue. That is when I notice he isn't a dwarf: the bottom of his legs have been cut off, he balances himself on a pair of uneven stumps.

"You think you're a big man walking around with your original legs, don't you, pretty boy?" He pulls out a pair of knives with an inwardly curved edge. "Wait 'til the worms get you. We'll see if you stay pretty." Tulbahadur inched his knives at me, and I pull back. "Look at yourself. You won't stand a chance. There's no fight in you."

I go red with anger again, mouth off, and shove the little guy against the bar stools. He goes down, but jumps back on his stumps like nothing happened. Tulbahadur wobbles up to me, and pulls back a wrinkled grin that cuts his snout in half. I can tell he gets off with the idea of an all-out brawl.

Leroy steps in between us, "Let's all relax; we don't want any trouble."

I try to simmer down and ignore the little guy, so I sidestep around him. Tulbahadur calls me a pussy and spits an ice cube down the hole in the back of my head. The burn gives me a mean head freeze.

We take a couple of stools at the other end of the bar to avoid any more bad business with that hostile little fucker. I'm on a mission here. I have to concentrate. This is all about Lorraine.

The television set hangs right over our heads. I crane my neck to make out what plays on the screen. All I can make out is some live footage of a race, the same one playing in my room, and all over this place. A scramble of players scale up the walls of the planetary core and try to reach the top of the rock sky. Every time one of them goes down the whole the bar goes wild.

Leroy approaches the bookie, a spectacled old man hunchbacked over the register, "We're looking for the Sybil."

The bookie looks up at him, his lips wedged shut with black stitches. He croaks through the neck-tie slit across the length of his throat, "Long time no see, Leroy. Who's your pal?"

"Don't mind him. He's just another noob," Leroy says.

The bookie drools through his neck wound, "She's getting her beauty sleep. It'll be a while. How about a drink while you wait?"

The bartender slides a couple of shots our way. She's pretty. The girl's got a crooked, livewire smile. Black lipstick that matches her one eye. The left side of her face melts into a mess of scar tissue and exposed bone. Her skull is hollowed out with a big, gaping hole on its side. I wonder if she used the gun on herself. If she's a suicide just like me.

Leroy shoots both our drinks and turns to the bookie, "How's the other side treating you?"

"You know… Still dead," he grumbles.

51

"Just because we're dead doesn't mean we can't have a little fun," Leroy reminds him.

"You got that right." The bookie's tongue unrolls out of his throat hole. "That's why we got the rock jockeys up there. Death's a waste without the races."

"Who looks good today?"

"I'd bet on Tulbahadur for the win," He points at the little guy. "He's a tough little bastard. Worked as a Himalayan Sherpa when he was living. He thinks that gives him an edge over the rest. This one will climb to at least ten thousand feet, I guarantee it. He fights dirty. Those kukri knives of his can be deadly up there. The fucker's small, but feisty."

Leroy places a bet on the Sherpa and gets another round of drinks for himself. He can't see a thing, but he wants to stand in front of the television set, capturing the noise and static, some kind of blind man radar. The players on the screen climb up the rock sky with pickaxes and grappling hooks. Another one drops and the crowd starts hooting.

I turn to Leroy, "What the fuck is a rock jockey?"

"There comes a point in every corpse's afterlife when you look up at that stone sky and think to yourself, 'Maybe I can climb out of this shit-hole; maybe I can ride the rock.' Some of the rock jockeys have gone pro and do it for the money or pussy. But most of them are just like you and me. Fed up. They've had enough of this place. And they want out, one way or another. So they play the game, and try to climb back up to their graves."

"Has anybody ever made it back there?"

"Who cares?" he shoots another drink, "The point isn't betting on who climbs the highest, but on when they're going to fall."

I look back at the waitress. She's got her good side turned to me. Her one black eye, inky as the grave. I mime giving a revolver a blowjob, and show her the hole in the back of my head. She laughs and winks at me.

"What caliber," I ask

"Forty five," She says.

My revolver was a scrawny little twenty two. Nothing more than a pop. Her weapon sounds serious, something that could do some real damage. It gives her an air of danger that I can't help envy. I pull out my chest, and lie to her about the size of the heat I had packing.

The bookie interrupts us; his tongue licks at the slit on his throat, "The Sybil is ready for you."

CHAPTER TEN

THE SYBIL

The ground moves shiftily, crawling with a nest of centipedes. We follow a set of stone cut steps, going deeper into the catacombs. There are more tunnels down here. They spread everywhere; a network of thousands of mines and passageways. The structure is huge. It doesn't seem to have an end—snaking through the earth in a side-wind, forming a complex ant colony. Who knows how long the dead have been down here digging. It looks like an eternity.

"Hurry up. She's waiting," Leroy disappears into the mouth of a cave.

I take a step inside. The rock lights up, alive with lichen and neon green moss. Fireflies swarm all around me. They tickle me, blinking on and off. Thick, burrowing roots dig through the earth, reach out, and coil gently around my fingers.

It feels hot in here. Sweat dribbles down my back. My suit sticks to me. The humidity only gets worst the deeper I go. I catch up with Leroy at the source of the heat, a hot spring steaming at the end of the cave.

Vapor rises in waves; its smell earthy and mineral. A group of men light a row of candles around the edge of the water, half-concealed by the smoke. They are stripped down to nothing but their undies. Their angel lust boners tent against the fabric.

Every one of their necks looks broken. Some of them hold their heads upright with neck braces. Others let them free to dangle. I can see the rope-burns, the broken bones tenting against their skin, the eyeballs crackled with veins. These men have all hung from a rope. They are suicides, men condemned for execution, autoerotic asphyxiation enthusiasts. Those erections are a dead giveaway—the lewd symptom of a burst in blood pressure, the snapping of the spine, suffocation, and sudden death.

One of the hanged men approaches us. He wears a steel neck brace with pins drilled into his skull. His erection bobs up and down as he bows.

"Point that thing someplace else," Leroy says.

The hanged man places his index finger between his lips. He points to a bed pushed back into a corner of the cave.

Something roils on the bed. And it is big. Two king-size mattresses can barely hold it. The thing stirs under a thick, furry blanket. It yawns, stretching out in the dark. Six hands cast shadows that warp against the rock.

"I know why you are here," the Sybil's voice carries through the chamber, "Which one of you is it? Show yourself to me. Who is this thief? This dead thing that wants to go poaching for souls."

I don't trust this moment. My knees start to shake. I'm about to piss myself. I start to backtrack, but Leroy pushes me towards her bed.

"That would be me," I mumble.

The Sybil looms over me. She's more than a big woman; she is three of them. The Sybil's a Siamese triplet. Every one of the old girls looks morbidly obese, bellies big enough that they roll over their privates. Clotted blood clusters under the skin of their ribs—the result of some massive, synchronized cardiac explosion. The triplets fuse together at the head, sharing a camber-shaped, alien skull.

The women cradle a star nosed mole in their arms. They pass it around in a constant circle. Each one of the triplets takes her turn petting the mole's albino fur, nuzzling it to sleep.

They speak, one head after the other, echoing each other's words, sharing sentences that stretch out like a bad speech impediment, "You are the one who wants me to pluck a ripe fruit from the living tree? Dig through the earth and drag her soul screaming to the other side."

"Yes. I need to see her again. Her name is Lorraine. I don't know where she is up there. But I have a piece of her hair." I take out the ribbon of hair from my pocket and hand it to her.

The Sybil's faces frown under a cake of foundation; her mouths purse into heart-shaped puckers. She snaps her fingers; every one of her six hands makes the same repetition. Her broken-necked boys catch her meaning, spring into action, and roll her bed to the hot springs.

The triplets untie the ribbon and spread Lorraine's hair in a sheet of foil. They spark up a lighter and burn the underside of the aluminum. The Sybil inhales the smoke, hoovering it into her lungs. Her ribcage expands—veins thicken, purple with old blood.

She exhales a column of smoke. It comes out from her three heads. The black cloud hovers over the spring. The smoke plunges into the water, rock-solid, taking the shape of an egg. It cracks open as it hits bottom. The shell breaks apart and leaks thick, sprawling oil. The water begins to boil.

The Sybil's eyes roll back and go white. The triplets levitate from the bed and hover over the bubbling spring. The mole orbits around them.

Lorraine surfaces from the spring, sucking for air. She comes out naked. Her skin scalded red by the boiling water. Saliva trickles from the sides of her lips. The hearts tattooed around her jugular beat hard and afraid.

She reaches out from the bubbling pool, "Help me!"

I drop to the edge of the spring and offer her my hand, "Lorraine. Give me your hand."

She turns her eyes on me. They widen. Her head begins to shake.

"Don't you recognize me? It's me. You're safe now. We're together again."

"No!" she screams.

"I've been waiting for you. But you never showed. We had a date remember?"

Lorraine pulls away from me; she paddles back into the water, "This isn't happening…"

"The plan was simple. I was going to eat the gun first; then you would follow. You said you wanted to watch me die so you would have no more reason to go on living."

"You are not real," she says, trying to convince herself.

"Why didn't you come after me?"

She doesn't answer, so I ask again.

Lorraine avoids looking me in the eye, "Do you really want to know…?"

"Tell me."

"I wasn't going to die; not for you," she says.

"Were you afraid?"

"I wasn't afraid…"

"I don't understand," I whisper this so it stays between us, "This whole thing was your idea."

She sighs, "It was the only way you would let me go. We had been together for far too long."

"What?"

"I was never going to follow you down here. You had to die so I could go on living."

"I don't believe it," I shake my head like a fool.

Lorraine's jaw sinks, half submerged in the water, "Don't play dumb with me, Bloom. You knew it was coming. There was nothing left between us."

"You tricked me."

She turns her back to me, "What do you want me to tell you? You were always ripe to die. All you needed was an excuse, one little push, another gloomy Sunday."

The cave shakes. An explosion goes off outside. I hear screams and a boom of noise. We all look back. One of the hanged boys rushes out from the tunnel yelling, "Raid!"

A swarm of men in white uniforms and surgical masks follow him inside. They gun the kid down. His head explodes all over the floor, but his body keeps crawling until it reaches the edge of the spring. The hotel staff fans out inside of the cave. They surround us. Their high-powered rifles aim for kill shots.

The Sybil falls back and bounces on her bed. The mole goes down next. It hides under the covers.

Lorraine screams. The water spins in a whirlpool around her. Her body gets sucked back into the spring. I jump into the water and grab her arm, trying to swim against the currents, and drag her out. I hold on to her hard. I can't let her go. She still has questions to answer.

She fights me—scratches and claws, teeth gnashed, whipping her yellow mane. I try my best to keep my grip on her, but she elbows me in the face, and manages to slip away. She gets swallowed by the swirling waters, and disappears, returning to the world of the living.

A couple of heavies from the staff drag me out of the spring, and toss me on my back. Their rifles aim at my head. I cough out some water, and raise my hands. Lorraine's gone. I lost her.

Steps come up from the tunnel. The reaper walks into of the cave. He sports the same well-pressed suit he always wears on the beach. The brim of his Panama hat shades half of his face. Those cold, icy eyes of his have the spark of something primitive and dangerous.

A crew of hotel staff in hard hats come in behind him. They set up wires to plastic charges and glue them around the walls of the cave.

The reaper takes a drag from a cigarette; he blows out a cloud of crossbones with the smoke, "Good day for a dig, huh?"

Nobody says a thing. The cave goes quiet. All I can hear is the slap and tack of his shoes.

The old man walks circles around Leroy, "Mr. Thurgood Leroy, good to see you again. You're not involved in this bad business, are you?"

Leroy lowers his head; he won't face him, "Nope. You know me, I always keep it clean."

The reaper turns to the Sybil, "Girls, girls, girls, I'm so disappointed in you. You three know it better than most—communication with the living is forbidden."

"We were forced," the triplets stammer. "It was this man's obsession. This corpse has gone mad with lust for the living. He is sick with his infatuation over this live girl. You must believe us!"

"Of course, I believe you," the reaper's voice sounds comforting, the kind of voice you use to lullaby a madman to sleep, "You are a model guest here at Paradise Cove. Someone must have led you astray."

He points straight at me, "You... I knew you were trouble the moment I laid eyes on you, Mr. Bloom. Suicides are rarely well-adjusted individuals."

"That doesn't surprise me," My big mouth goes off again. The reaper smiles back at me, and I can't help but go cold.

"You are new here," he says, "and might not know how things work. In this underworld there are rules. You are given a paradise. All you have to do is enjoy it. Is that so hard?"

"You should spruce the place up then." I smirk.

"Paradise Cove is not up to your standards?"

"These catacombs are better than that shithole you got going on upstairs."

He closes in on me, "So, you like it down here, Mr. Bloom?

"It's not that bad. Maybe you should try it. The food looks great."

He blows a stream of smoke from his nostrils. It tightens around my neck in the shape of a black constrictor. "It doesn't surprise me that you like it down here. You corpses are all the same: can't help but answer the call to the ground. You feel right at home buried six feet under, don't you? Or do you like it deeper?"

"Now that I'm a rotted corpse, I'll try anything."

"If you like it underground so much, maybe you should stay here for a while," he turns to the staff, "I want this place leveled. Blow the charges."

The staff scrambles in the background. Leroy cradles into a ball on the ground. The Sybil keeps screaming that she's innocent. Her broken-necked boys take cover wherever they can. The mole is already tunneling the hell out.

Someone starts a countdown. The reaper winks at me as he hits the detonator. A fireball spreads out through the cave. The structure shakes and the earth comes crashing down us.

Chapter Eleven

Dinner Time

Who knows how long I've been buried down here... There's nothing but darkness all around me. Time doesn't exist without a glimpse at the light.

I lie flat on my stomach, my body pinned between the earth and a slab of rock. The soil settles around me. Its weight keeps constant pressure on my bones. I can't take it. The load is too much to bear. My leg snaps. Ribs break in a chain, one after the other. A fissure cracks across the dome of my skull. I scream out from the pain and swallow a mouthful of dirt.

My neck feels dislocated. I'm pretty sure my head's twisted upside down. I nestle into a pillow of bedrock, but can't quite get comfortable. My skin tingles with microbial activity. Bacteria break down my soft tissue and leave me covered in a slick, stinking slime. It hardens into a jam between my toes. I can smell it. The rot has set in.

Suddenly, I hear them out there: a wet, oozing reverb. The sound of their bodies wriggling in the soil sends shivers up my spine. I feel them moving around on their bellies, crawlers slicking the ground with their slime. Worms.

Shit. I keep quiet. Don't move a muscle. Play dead. But my body betrays me. It melts away. Leaks its gases. The stink riles the crawlers. They catch my scent, and speed up their digging.

The worms get to me in no time. I can feel their snouts sniffing at my skin. They're checking out the quality of my meat, making sure that my body's nice and putrefied, just the way they like it.

I buck around and try to shake them off, but they just keep on coming: there are too many.

Dinnertime. They munch on me. Take big, greedy bites, and open a hole through my gut. The worms slip inside. They slither past my organs, sliding on the wet tissue. The parasites reach the intestinal wall and chew through it. They snuggle together in a pile near the colon, sharing the heat, and laying their eggs.

I scream alone in the dark.

I try to stop struggling. Stay still and let it happen. Save myself the pain—the fucking embarrassment. But the worms get harder to ignore. They keep growing, tenting my stomach. Some of them are getting too big to slide into the small intestine. Those have settled somewhere around my rectum. They explore through the cavity and pop out for air.

Space is getting scarce in there. There isn't room for all of them. Tempers get short. The worms turn violent. Fights for living space break out all the time. Only the very big ones survive. I can hear them hiss, wrestle, and bite—go at each other, and eat the remains.

It's getting harder and harder not to go insane down here. I try to keep her in my mind. Lorraine is all I have left. I remember her heart-shaped tattoos. The bounce of her ass as she stepped into the tub. Her wet body. The way she held the gun. Her fucking lies to me. I need to focus on my hate, the demons in my blood, on her, on something real outside this worm infested horror show. Otherwise, I will lose my motherfucking mind.

I reach into my pocket to get a feel of her hair, but stop myself, remembering that it is long gone. It went up in smoke.

I want to forgive you. Let you move on with your life. Be an adult about this. But who is kidding who? I don't know how to do that.

CHAPTER TWELVE

PAROLED

They dig me out of the ground. My body rolls out on the beach, coughing up mud and dirt. I crawl around trying to get on my feet, but only manage to fall back on my ass.

The reaper stands over me. He dusts off dirt from one shoe with the heel of the other. The old man reaches into his suit and pulls out some wet knaps.

He hands me a wad of tissues, "Clean yourself up."

The hotel staff scrambles in the background. A couple of excavators sift through the earth looking for bodies. They pile the debris into neat sandcastle pyramids. Leroy and the Sybil get dug up next. He plops on the ground and dusts himself off. She hangs from one of the cranes, screaming for her pet mole.

"How are you boys feeling?" the reaper asks.

"Peachy," Leroy says, "A little decomp doesn't hurt anyone. It builds character. Are we free to go?"

"You're on parole with restrictions on poolside drinks and use of the clubhouse until further notice," the reaper lights a cigarette. "Mr. Leroy, you know the drill. Gentlemen if you please, get on your hands and knees. The staff will begin the deworming procedure when you are in position."

The worms roil in my stomach. I bend over and stick my ass into the air, breathing heavy, my teeth gritted.

"I'll see you on the beach, boys," the reaper smiles. "Don't miss out. The water looks lovely today."

Chapter Thirteen

Bio-fetish

I lay back on the sand, getting roasted by the planetary core. Radiation buzzes on my lips. It licks at me with a sizzle—burns at the touch. I open my mouth and let it seep inside of me, but it tastes like nothing.

I look around at the corpses crowding the beach. They play cards, build sandcastles, squirt lotion on each other, get loaded, and pass out on their tanning chairs. They seem perfectly happy in this half-assed paradise. Everybody here is just wasting time, chasing after this fake sun.

Leroy takes the shade under a palm tree. He sips on one of those pink cocktails, swirling around the little umbrella.

"So," I ask, "what's our next move?"

"Our move?" He does a spit take, "I'm out of your crazy bio-fetish adventures. You're on your own."

"We're not done yet," I grab on to his coat. "Lorraine's still out there. That girl owes me."

He pushes me away, "You're obsessed with this live girl. What's so hot about the living, anyway? A warm slit and breathing heavy are overrated. You want my advice. Get yourself a nice, cold corpse. You're in the right place for it."

"She can't get away with this, Leroy," I gnash my teeth, "I can't let it go."

"You did die a chump…"

"She tricked me," I correct him.

"Your girl is probably in someone else's bed, sweating with another man. That makes you a chump in my book." He pats my shoulder. "But don't worry about it. You are not the only one. This sort of thing happens all the time. Our loved ones have a habit of dealing us double."

I don't want to admit it, but he's right. She made a fool of me. But my death isn't all on her. The thing is suicide always made sense to me. I always thought I was meant to kill myself. Take matters into my own hands. Jump ahead of the line. Get the hell out of the world. It was in my fucking blood. I might have been tricked into it, but the idea has always been there, rooted in the back of my brain, calling me to the other side.

The hole in the back of my head prickles. I reach over and scratch at the bullet's exit wound. Every time I touch it the opening seems to be getting larger.

"You're right, I am a chump," I take a sip from his drink. "Lorraine promised me we would cross over to the other side to be together. She fooled me into shooting myself just to get rid of me. Now I'm a prisoner in this shitty resort. And I just had my insides raped and Swiss-cheesed by a colony of worms. That girl deserves my revenge."

"What are you going to do about it…?" he shrugs.

"I want to go back, crossover, climb the rock sky, and hunt the world for her. She won't be able to hide from me. I will chase her down. Corner her like some animal."

"Then what?" he asks.

I close in on him, "I'm going to possess her. She will never be able to leave me again."

"Let me get this straight," Leroy says. "You want to play in the rock jockey races, climb back up to your grave, find that Lorraine bitch, and possess the shit out of her?"

"Yes."

"You'll be a longshot. I could make a killing on you with the bookie…" he pretends to think it over, "I like it. I'm in."

I take another sip off his cocktail, "I've been meaning to ask you something."

"Here it goes…" He takes his drink back.

"How did you die?"

Leroy puffs up his chest, "Drive by shooting."

"That sounds exciting," I sound a little too impressed.

"Not really," he deflates back to his original size, "It wasn't exactly a drive by shooting, more of a drive-in sort of shooting."

"What do you mean?"

"I had just picked up this girl at the mall. She was an itty bitty little thing, but packed a punch where it counted. I had my eye on that ass for a while. You see, I was bit of a player back then. Had a pulse and everything.

"I took her to get some of those hard shell taquitos. I was in my car, minding my own business, ordering at the Taco Max drive-through window, getting a hand job—you know, living the life. That's when she caught me. Anita was watching from the security cameras."

"Who's Anita?"

"Anita was my wife. I had no idea she had just taken a job at that Taco Max. When I pulled over to pay at the register she was waiting for me with her momma's old double-barrel pistol drawn.

The gun looked like some penny arcade bullshit toy. It only held a single bullet in each chamber. But Anita was a hell of a shot. She popped me once, then twice, and I was a goner."

Leroy takes off his sunglasses. Both his eyeballs are gone— the sockets scorched black, darkness reaches back into his skull.

CHAPTER FOURTEEN

ROCK JOCKEYS

We trek down the coastline until we hit the chain-link fence at the far end of the resort. Footprints lie etched on the sand. They lead to a hidden trail that snakes between the sand dunes and ends at the mouth of another tunnel.

Leroy smiles wide, and says he's going to keep watch.

I go in first, crawling on all fours, splashing through the slop of water swamped inside. A brood of leeches catches my scent as I pass. They rise to the surface of the puddle, and latch on to my body. The leeches wriggle over my clothes, struggling to find a way into the suit. But they're crafty suckers, single-minded; they squirm around, and probe, and discover a breach through the zipper.

The parasites latch on to the sweet spots on my body: the pits, at the back of my knees, and the warm clefts between my thighs. They take my blood in slurps, sucking greedily like they haven't fed for an eternity. But suddenly they stop. The leeches begin to burp and heave. They peel their wet maws from my skin, and retch.

I laugh out loud at the suckers. Serves them right. My blood's too old for them. I'm way past my expiration date. The leeches drop back into the water, and don't bother me again.

I manage to squeeze through and come out on the other side of the fence—on the edge of the fucking world.

Leroy follows me out of the tunnel, and pats my shoulder, "There it is, Bloom."

A black mountain range spreads out in front of me. It stretches over the horizon. The cliffs look impossible; the rocks jagged and sharp. Massive columns of basalt and igneous rock rise up in a vertical sweep. The slabs of hardened magma support the weight of the dome looming above our heads.

I can't help but take a step back. The height of the range overwhelms me. It plays strange tricks on my mind. The mountains seem to keep on growing, they get bigger and bigger until they swallow everything around them.

Leroy shows me the way to base of the mountains. Something of a large tailgate party is in full swing down here. The fans have built themselves a nice set up to watch the races. Golf carts circle each other in a wagon train. Meat gets charcoaled on makeshift cinderblock grills. Keggers cool on salted ice. Music plays from rivaling speakers wired to go-cart batteries. A large bonfire burns right smack in the middle of the caravan.

Nobody takes their eyes off the mountains. The race has the fans worked up. They jump from their foldout chairs, and gasp loudly with every close call. A few girls bare their tits at the players going up on the rock. Boys with painted faces howl around drunk, and beat their chest with their buddies. They roll in packs, and chant their favorite rock jockeys names, picking fights with each other easy.

The professional rock jockeys are not difficult to spot up there. They put on a show and make wild jumps between the cliffs, launch into these high-risk spins, and wave their banners from the mountainside. Anything to call the attention of the fans or the cameras. The jockeys wear these bizarre, sparkling costumes; a patchwork of sequins, Lycra, loud polyesters, and lace. They look like Mexican wrestlers in gaudy showgirl drag.

Cameramen take footage of the races from the guard towers on the other side of the resort's fence. I can tell from their white uniforms, and their perfect, coiffed hair that they are Paradise Cove staff. I wave at them, but they don't answer back.

Most of the corpses out here for the races don't look like pros. Not by a longshot. They are just regular stiffs. They don't care much about the cameras. These folks just want to get back home. They travel in groups. Entire families carry their belongings in plastic bags. Some of them pull on carts and saddle the carcasses of dead mules, taking the crowded road that leads through the mountain pass.

All these desperate, stumbling corpses have the feel of a pilgrimage. Or better yet, an exodus. An illegal migration, the population exchange of a zombie horde. Priests and snake charmers sell blessings at every crossroads.

I spot Tulbahadur in the middle of the crowd. The little guy has an entourage of dead girlies crouching all over him to match his size. He pulls out a sharpie, and signs his autograph on their cleavage. The Sherpa is in full get-up for the race. Tulbahadur painted his face with camouflage makeup, and looks pretty badass wearing Kevlar and fatigues under his shaggy, albino fur.

He looks up and meets my gaze. The little fucker has mean eyes. The Sherpa hocks a wad of spit into the sand. He cracks his knuckles, bends the bones on his neck.

I wink at him, and throw him back a kiss. The little guy wobbles on his stumps, and throws himself at me, but his girlies hold him back.

73

Leroy smacks me on the bullet hole in the back my head, "Concentrate! It's going to be a hell of a climb. No one would blame you if you turned tail and went back to your bungalow. Getting through that mountain range is only the first obstacle. Once you trek the mountains, you'll have to scale the columns of volcanic rock. Nobody's ever made that climb."

I tilt my head and look up at the rock sky. I say it, but I am not sure if I really mean it, "I'll make it…"

"If you manage to reach the top, then it starts getting tricky," he says. "You have to fight gravity and crawl on the dome itself to go up through one of its cracks. Once you're in the earth all you have to do is dig around for a coffin and ride it back home."

"Have you ever tried the climb?" I ask.

"No way. I've lost too many body parts already," He slides his shades up his nose. "There's no talent in dropping."

"But it's possible? Can I climb up the grave and get back home?"

"I've never seen it."

"You're blind."

"That is also true."

Lorraine lingers in the back of my mind. She laughs, taunting at me with the revolver. Spins the chamber and spills out the bullet cases. They are shaped like tiny caskets. Little versions of my corpse are stuffed into every one of the shells.

I make up my mind, and run towards the mountains.

I am coming for you. Can you feel it? My breath on the back of your neck. Me scratching and tearing to get in. Your sweet refusals. My fingers hooked on your soul, playing your body like a marionette.

CHAPTER FIFTEEN

GRATEFUL FOR
EVERY DAMNED BITE

The procession moves slowly through the mountain pass. I mix in with the rest of the pilgrims and watch the crowd grow bigger and bigger. Fresh bodies keep on coming, bottlenecking the only gap through the rock.

A row of stone-cut minarets juts out from the mountainside. The pilgrims gather around them, and reach out, begging for a blessing from the priests, monks, imams, and snake charmers on top of the turrets. The snake charmers are the most popular; the crowd goes for them in droves. The charmers hide their faces behind layers of ragged veils, and offer their blessings with vipers coiled up their arms. Their animals look drugged—slow and graceless, eyes as big as saucers. The snake charmers milk the poison straight from the reptile's fangs and spray the venom into the crowd.

The pilgrims and rock jockeys open their mouths wide. They push and fight and topple over each other—everybody desperate for a taste. The pilgrims go down with seizures, roll into fits in the sand, talk nonsense and call it speaking in tongues.

I join in and lap at the venom. Drink the reptile's poison in gulps. It spills out in a gush from the sides of my mouth. The venom numbs everything it touches as it slides down my throat. It rushes right through me. The high is strong—hits me like a sledgehammer, peels my eyes wide open, boosts me with an uptick of stamina. My body feels alive again; the wound in the back of my head sealed shut and perfectly healed.

There is nothing but bodies up ahead. I've got a long haul coming my way. This is it. There is no turning back. I have to brace myself and man up.

A pile of severed body parts rises at the base of the mountain: smashed skulls, whole legs, and flailing torsos—the remains of the fallen rock jockeys. Twisted bodies move in a crabwalk, bones sticking out like horns through the skin. Crawlers drag behind ropes of their own innards.

I follow the rest of the pilgrims up the main trail. I let them guide me. They have a collective memory, a mind hive bonded out of shared experiences. These amateur rock jockeys know the best roads, shortcuts, hidden passes…the right trails that cut through the range.

I have a good pump going. The snake poison booms in my bloodstream, and just begins to peak. My body feels amped. Reflexes on a hair trigger. Ready for anything. I can feel it: luck is with me, and I'm going to need it.

We trek up a switchback path that meanders the side of the mountain. The trail gets steeper and narrows the higher we climb. It leads to a network of caves that tunnel through the rock, and reaches up to the summit where a straggling, flat mesa overlooks the ocean.

A rope bridge swings with the wind over the sprawling canyon that stands between us and the next peak. It looks rickety.

The bridge's wooden boards don't seem safe; termite holes pockmark every slat. They look about to give in.

I step in line and follow the queue to go over the crossing. The boards screech with every step I take, but just I swallow hard, and keep on moving.

The flow of traffic slows on the bridge. I wait around, looking down at the abyss. But something is wrong. The planks I'm standing on feel weak, almost hollow. About to give in. New cracks run through the wood. The planks splinter apart with my weight, snap in two, and collapse off the bridge. I fall through the broken boards, but manage to hold on to the load-bearing rope. The bridge swings violently with the wind, rocking my body from side to side.

I look back and realize that I am jamming traffic on the bridge. The pilgrims scream at me, and toss rocks, bottles, and aluminum cans to hurry me up. A few of them go over the rail with all the swinging. I pull myself back on the bridge and get going again, feeling dizzy and desperate until I make it to the other side.

I collapse on my hands and knees when I reach solid ground. Faces look down on me: rock cut heads carved on the mountaintop—every one of them screams. I study the sculptures up close, finger their gaping mouths, the irregular edges of the teeth, and try to imitate the terror etched on their faces.

The pilgrims keep together, and set up camp. They light cook fires, boil canned beans, and pass around salted meats. Drink moonshine that tastes like pickle juice. Teach each other how to flintknap Stone Age tools with wood, antlers, and smoothed-out bone. The pilgrims take care of the dead kids making the climb alone. Share their family tents with total strangers. They sit around the fires and tell stories to each other. Reveal the things they've seen; the wonders out there. Lower their voices at the talk of more hells.

These stiffs lean on each other. Help themselves up when they fall. I wonder how long all this love between them is going to last.

I warm up next to one of the cook fires and cozy up with the flames. My body aches all over. I feel beat up. Tired. I close my eyes, and do my best to drift off, but I can't do it; nothing clicks into fucking place. I keep on forgetting that I'm a dead. Sleep is something alien to me now.

I decide to go for a walk. Most of the pilgrims keep close to the fires, so I have the whole top of the mountain all to myself. I find a nice, lonely spot, and plop down, letting my legs hang off the edge of the cliff. Looking out into the horizon, I can barely make out the tiny sparks of light from the tailgate party at the base of the range; the flicker from their grills and barbeques.

That's when I spot Tulbahadur again. The little guy sits on a rise, kicking pebbles down the side of the mountain. He turns his head over his shoulder and locks eyes with me.

The Sherpa wobbles over and scoots next to me on the edge of the cliff, "What do you think you are doing up here?"

"The same as everybody else. Trying to get the fuck out of this place."

His snout splits into a crooked smile. "Let me give you a word of advice. Save yourself the trouble."

"Why's that?"

"You see all these good people here?" He makes a sweeping hand gesture in the direction of the pilgrims' encampment. "Not one of them is going to climb near a thousand feet. It is a waste

78

of time. These poor bastards only came here to drop. They don't have it in them. And neither do you."

"We'll see about that…" I mutter.

"Look at yourself," He pokes at my chest with his finger. "What makes you think you can make it? Those legs of yours are a handicap—two fucking anchors. They will only weigh you down at the end. You are not going to make it up there. Nobody will."

"Not even you?"

"Oh, I'll make it…someday. This is my seven-hundred-and-fifty-third try up this sucker. Every time I ride the rock I climb a little bit higher. It's all a matter of time and patience, but I'm going to inch myself back to my fucking grave. Whatever it takes…

"The climb used to be more of a struggle, when I had more weight on me. But I am nothing if not committed. I lost those extra pounds in a snap." He pulls up his fatigues and shows me his stumps. "I buried my legs in the earth and fed them to the worms. They took a huge load off me, and I was grateful for every damned bite."

"You are one crazy bastard," I blurt out.

"If you're really serious about wanting to get out of here, get bold, get lighter." Tulbahadur pulls out his curved kukri knifes. "All you have to do is ask me to start cutting."

CHAPTER SIXTEEN

THE CLIMB

By the time we make it out of the mountains things start to get nasty pretty quickly. It becomes a mad scramble. A violent race towards the columns of volcanic rock that lead up to the dome. The pilgrims go crazy. They trample over each other, clawing, beating back anybody who stands between them and the vertical climb. The knives come out. Arms and legs get cut loose. Heads lopped off. Bodies torn to pieces. Families broken apart. Every man and woman is now on their own.

The professional rock jockeys hold back, and let the pilgrims go at each other first. They let them take care of themselves. Bring down the numbers. The jockeys only go in when the field looks almost cleared; they mow down the last standing bodies and leap onto the volcanic rock.

I follow behind the jockeys, using them as a shield, weaving through the remaining pilgrims to reach the base of the massive columns.

They look over me, and spiral into the sky. I get a firm hold on the rock and start to climb. I feel my way up the surface, fingering the nooks and crannies, and anchoring my heels on the irregular features warping the face of the volcanic rock.

Higher up the column, the surface is carved with rows upon rows of rock cut rungs—a vertical sweep of ladders that lead up to the dome. My fingers slot into each groove, and fit into them like they were made for me. These defiles on the sides of the column are all that's left of everyone that went before me. An eternity of souls scrambling to get out of hell and all they have to show for it are these scratch marks carved on the rock.

I climb bareback. Bare hands on the rock. I take it one step at a time, making sure I got a good hold of one rung, before I reach out for the next. I take a look around and size up the completion. Some of the other climbers seem more prepared than me. They use makeshift crampons, grappling hooks, harnesses, hammers and spikes to steady themselves as they climb up the columns. I didn't plan a thing. I just improvised my way up here. They make me feel like a rookie, and a fool.

Some of the pilgrims climb in groups, a chain of human bodies. Most go at it alone. A few decide against the impossible and rappel down the rock.

Above me, a mess of bodies dangles from the side of the column. The professional rock jockeys stand out among the rest. Their costumes sparkle; streamers flare with the wind. They do high-risk spins, and pirouettes on the upper tiers, drawing gasps and clapping from the crowd of fans below.

It feels like I'm getting up there. The air turns thin. I can longer see solid ground. I keep on going—zero in on my target. All there is lies above me: the rock sky.

The wind cracks against me. I grip at the rungs and my arms tense with the strain. My muscles feel weak—about to give in. I want to stop for a while and rest. Close my eyes. But I can't lose the momentum. If I stop I fall.

The planetary core rotates above me. Its heat starts getting to me. Sweat pours down my face. Tongue goes sandpaper dry. My whole body feels cooked by the radiation. I start losing my clothes to cool myself down, funerary jacket, pants, and the dress shirt, throwing them off the abyss. All I got left is my undies and a tie. The naked jockey. I might just get famous.

I am getting closer. I can feel it. Nothing can stop me now. My grave is still warm and waiting for me. Lorraine's got no idea what she's got coming.

The rock jockeys start to play hardball. The motherfuckers throw a barrage of boulders and debris aimed straight at the amateurs below. Most of the rock slide misses me, but I get slimed with something wet on the face: some of those bastards up there got their cocks out and piss down the side of the column.

Bodies drop like flies all around me. The pilgrims get knocked out by another salvo of boulders. One of them gets his head flattened by a torpedo shaped slab; his bloody body swoops down right next me, almost taking me down with him. One fucking heart-stopper of a close call.

Another rock flies at me. I roll out of its way before it hits, and watch it smash into pieces against the column. The rock jockey lobbing the stones at me hangs one-handed from just a few stories above. He glares at me from behind his camouflage makeup. It's Tulbahadur. The Sherpa pulls back a sneer, and hurls another rock at me.

I dodge out of the way, "You missed, mother fucker!"

Tulbahadur keeps throwing down rocks at me, cursing in his native tongue. His little stumps flail in a childish tantrum when he misses. I dodge and weave, jumping from one ladder to the next to dodge the incoming barrage.

Luck is with me. He keeps missing. This little bastard has it in for me. He tries to knock me down with all he's got. Tulbahadur gets winded, but keeps on going. He can't stop himself. Something keeps him going. Smoke puffs from his nostrils, slips out from his mouth, his eyeballs turn black with an angry cloud; a darkness takes a hold of him. I recognize that darkness as my own.

Tulbahadur isn't going to stop unless I make him stop. This will only end when one of us drops. A cloud of dark smoke riles inside of me to match his own. I have to man up to this moment if I'm going to make it out of here. So I pick up my pace and climb up to his level.

I scramble up to where he's perched and try to get a hold of him, but the little guy is quick, nimble, and difficult to catch. He swings from the rungs, climbing higher and higher, the yeti fur off his back bristled. I reach out to catch him, but he smacks me with a rock in the face.

I spit out a wad of blood, and lunge at him, snag onto his fur and pull him back to me. His stumps flail and kick at my groin. He pushes away from me, nails reaching to pop my eyeballs. I close a tense, white knuckled fist, and break his nose.

Tulbahadur starts to shriek. The little guy throws himself at me, and we wrestle up and down the ladder. Swiping at each other. Trading punches. The fucker goes at me with a vengeance. He claws and bites, tries to choke me with my tie. The Sherpa pulls out his curved kukri knives and goes on a mad stabbing spree. Smoke spills out from his mouth. He looks zoned out— eyes fucking spinning with violence.

I get stabbed about a dozen times in my chest and belly before I manage to get him off me, smash my fist into his snout, and knock him overboard.

But Tulbahadur doesn't go down easy, the fucker latches on to my leg; he stabs me at the calf with his kukri knives. The Sherpa weighs me down. I can barely hold on to the rungs.

The nibs of my fingers claw on the rock, break the skin, and draw blood. I slip, and drop before I know it. Don't even have time to scream.

Everything around me spins in a whirl. Gravity crushes at my body. The noise of the fans at the base of the mountains boom and rises. Their shouting reverbs off the volcanic rock. I hear the crowd go wild as I crash-land to the ground.

The cameras loom over me; I can feel the heat off their lenses. The fucking vultures swarm around my body.

Things don't look good. I can't get up. My body feels odd, warped; like it's been flattened. A couple of broken ribs stab through my chest. My head rests on the balls of my feet. One of my eyeballs dangles from the optical nerves, and rasps against the sand.

I see him coming from my popped out eyeball. A trail of smoke wriggles behind him in the shape of a tail that ends in a loud, black rattle. The reaper kneels down to my level and picks up my eye from the ground. He blows the mites of sand off the cornea and plugs the whole thing back into my socket.

"Are we having fun yet?" the reaper asks.

CHAPTER SEVENTEEN

GONE COLD BLOODED

Back on the beach, the sun sizzles on my skin. I stretch out and yawn, taking a sip of my pink cocktail. Lazing around here isn't that bad. My tan's just getting going, and I am working up a base for an even bronze. The planetary core's radiation feels like nothing but goodness.

Leroy sits on the tanning chair next to mine. He's in a mood, talking trash about how much money he lost on me on the rock jockey races.

"You didn't even make it to a hundred feet." He parrots the same thing over and over. "That was bad even for a first try."

I look out at the beach, turn both ways, and see nothing but dead bodies cooking in either direction. They laze about, tanning and enjoying the spike in temperature, just like me. There's no doubt about it. I have gone native. I'm just another one of the cold blooded guests here at Paradise Cove. Maybe I've been one of them all along, and never even realized it. I was never any good at being human.

"I have gone cold blooded," I mutter.

Leroy ignores me.

I sink back in the chair and finish my drink. A familiar feeling sweeps over me. Sweet, pleasing, telling me that this is the end of the road. There is nothing left for me. It is time to stop kidding myself. Nothing is going to get any better. I want to run away. Find an escape route. End this bullshit once and for all.

I'm not sad. Not really. I feel relieved. Suicide has always come easy for me. It's just another way to get away—self-medicate. Killing myself relieves the pressure. It takes the edge off.

I walk across the beach and swim into the ocean. The waves crash against me. I keep on going, swimming deeper and deeper, making sure that I can't get back to the shore. My arms and legs start to give. The muscles cramp, trembling from exhaustion. I let my body sink into the ocean and swallow a mouthful of water.

Nothing... It doesn't work. Every time I swallow the water bubbles out of the hole in the back of my head. I cover it with the palms of my hands and try again. My lungs balloon with water, but all I feel is sick from the salt.

I stay in the ocean for hours. Being stubborn about it. Eventually, Leroy drags me out by the back of my collar. I roll on the beach and let my clothes dry a bit. My skin paunches from the exposure to the water; strips of flesh peel off with a scratch.

Leroy slips under the shade of a palm tree and orders another round of cocktails. I decide to try and see if I can drink myself to death, but I don't have high hopes: I always had a talent for holding my liquor.

Chapter Eighteen

Coffin Riders

It takes me a couple of tries to stick my keycard into the slot. I burst back into my bungalow, stumbling around drunk, feeling my way through the walls for the light switch.

I trip on the rollers of the swivel chair, and fall flat on my face. Blood spurts out of my mouth, and pools beneath me. The ground goes slick with it. I try to get back on my own two feet, but don't make it on the first try.

It takes me awhile, but I manage to get bipedal again. It doesn't last long, though. Waves of drunken vertigo crash over me. I teeter around in a haze. My head doesn't stop spinning. Knees go weak and buckle. I slump on the swivel chair and spin around, going in the opposite direction of the ceiling fan. The fan buzzes over my head. I blink every time I spot the shape of the blades. I now know what I have to do.

I shake off the drunkenness, fight the stickiness cobwebbing through my body, and get out from the chair. My suit sticks to me, still wet and dripping saltwater. I struggle to slip out of the jacket, and then peel the shirt off my back. A couple of buttons pop loose. Even the zipper gives me trouble as I shimmy out of my pants. Necktie and undies stay on.

Water wrings from my tie with ever tightening Indian-burns. I fix the sloppy Windsor knot and tense it against my throat. It grows tighter, a balled up fist shutting the air flow. I slide the loop in a one-hundred-and-eighty degree turnabout until the knot secures at the nape of my neck. I hold up the wide end of the tie, and make a hangman's noose.

I flick the switch and watch the fan slow and stop. I get up on the swivel chair next, reach up, and secure the wide end of my necktie to the base of the fan. The swivel chair rocks back and forth until it tips over.

The noose tightens. Wet fabric squeezes around my throat. I gasp for breath. Eyeballs pop out. Pressure builds up in my skull. Something cracks. My head feels lighter, rushed with blood.

The thrill seems familiar, out of my old bag of tricks—that electric sensation of getting away with something. There's nothing like it.

«««—»»»

All I do is hang there for hours. My feet paddle like underwater. I count the wooden slats on the ceiling to pass the time. Suicide is getting tricky.

I hear the door creak open, but my back is turned. Steps close in on me. Someone flicks a switch, and starts up the ceiling fan. I start spinning around, my body picks up speed as the motor revs.

The reaper sits with his legs crossed on the swivel chair. He keeps sticking me with the tip of his shoe. The old man pokes at me the way you do at dead things—slightly disgusted, hoping they won't answer back.

I keep going round; the noose coiling up tighter and tighter.

"Go away. I'm busy here," I croak.

"Not again, Mr. Bloom? You suicides are such bad escape artists." He lights a cigarette.

"Mind your own business, reaper."

The old man shakes his head, "Poor fool…you are going down the wrong road. Death is not better the second time around. Never break that last seal if you don't have what it takes to make it on the other side. Don't you know where corpses go when they bite the big one? This is not the last hell in this underworld."

"I don't care where I go anymore," I mumble. "As long as it is out of this place."

"You are dead. It is a little late to get sentimental," His cold, icy eyes roll back.

"Fuck you!" I try to kick at the smug old man, but the ceiling fan keeps spinning, and making me miss.

The reaper half grins at me. He puffs out a cloud of smoke from the sides of his lips. It builds up in a cloud behind him, shape shifting into a chorus of sniggering skulls.

"Why do you let us make that ridiculous climb up that rock if all we can do is fall?" I ask him, screaming.

He shrugs his shoulder, and turns off the fan. "A little bit of hope helps keeps everybody in line."

The old man reaches into his suit. He pulls out a straight razor. The ivory handle gleams in the light as the blade springs loose—the razor curves in the shape of a scythe. The reaper puts the sharp end of the blade against my throat. His thumb presses on the spine of the steel and slices through my necktie, cutting me down from the ceiling fan.

I land on my ass, and take big, panicky breaths, "Kill joy…"

"You dead things are all the same," he says. "None of you can just grin and bear it. What makes you think your pain is so special? There are others just like you.

"Do you know how many of you drop down to this underworld? Your corpses are piling up. This place stinks of your rot. One day your diseases will consume us all."

"This place is one-way access," I scoff. "Don't pretend like you didn't get here in a coffin just like the rest of us."

The reaper grows angry; he closes in on me, smoke slipping from his clenched teeth, "I am the hand of death. A gatekeeper of souls. Warden of the first circle of hell. I have kept watch over the ancient ramparts of the last city of the dead, and stared back at the void. My black wings mean that this shadow world is mine to reap."

"Am I supposed to be impressed?"

He laughs, smoke morphs into a pair of black wings flared across his back, "You should be. Everybody has some monster lurking inside. Something bad in the blood. A darkness we hide out of fear of it taking us over. Only madmen have the balls to unleash the monster, and let it spread its wings.

"What about you, Mr. Bloom, do you have the balls to let the monster loose? Or are you no different than all the others? Just another carcass in the ground."

"I am not like the rest of those of rotted corpses out there."

"Aren't you?" He tears off a strip of dead skin and hair from the wound on the back of my head.

"You get used to it after a while," I shrug.

"Face it, Mr. Bloom; this is where you belong now."

"Look, I just want to go back home."

"To what?" he snorts. "That place you remember is long gone. Even if you could go back it would never be the same."

I shake my head, stubbornly, "You don't know that. You don't understand. This means everything to me. Lorraine is still out there. She and I have unfinished business. This is about love and revenge, old man. I won't ever stop."

"You have a restless soul. A wayfarer's one. So did I, once…" The old man meets my eyes and his features soften. "Tell me, Mr. Bloom, do you really want to get out of this place? Are you really ready to face a nightmare in the face just so you can try your luck at hunting your old girlfriend down?"

"I do. I want it bad." I sound like I'm begging for it. "But I can't make that climb. It's impossible. I tried…"

"There is another way out," he interrupts me. "I myself have wandered through the nine known hells, the realm of the living, and those dark places beyond."

My eyes widen, "Tell me."

"There's a price to pay. The journey will change you. It will show you who you really are. No doubt about it. The hells always reveal the monsters we hide underneath."

"What do I have to lose; I'm already dead, remember?"

He huffs his breath on the straight razor, making the blade fog, teasing out the tension, "You ever heard of a coffin rider?"

I shake my head.

"A coffin rider is a fugitive, an escaped soul. They are death runners. Jumpers between worlds. Ghosts that travel through the fluid spaces of the underworld. Abominations that can die more than one time."

"How can I learn this skill?"

"It's easy, really. There is not much to it. This ritual should be something familiar to the likes of you. Slit those wrists, Mr. Bloom. Kill yourself again and again, over and over, from one hell to the next, until you stumble back into world of the living."

The reaper's Panama hat tilts over one eye. He hands me the straight razor.

I hold the razor in my hands and run my finger on the sharp edge of the blade, "How long will it take me to get back home?"

He pats my shoulder, and grins like a jackal.

Sparks run up my arm as the blade cuts the skin for the first time: I'm cheating at death again. Blood pools out, and I brace myself for another ride down a crazy, motherfucking rabbit hole.

CHAPTER NINETEEN

LUST

I gasp for air like my lungs still work and belt out another scream. My body drops from another hair-raising height, but already begins to stall, and I lose altitude. I plunge into a dense, sprawling jungle, and rip through the green canopy, snapping branches and a web of straggling vines. The earth closes in on me, and I land on a briar patch that grows at the base of the trees.

The thorns nail in and crucify me to the thicket, arms and legs pulled apart. They lodge deep into my skin. The spikes finish in hooks, and anchor onto the meat. A whole hornet's nest of them sting all over my body. I pluck a single thorn out of my skin and wince from the pain. If I keep picking at them one by one I am going to be stuck here doing this all day; there are too many of them. I got to get unstuck quickly. The only way to do this is like I would a band-aid, in one painful wrench. Teeth gritted, I tear my body from the briar patch. Blood splatters on the soil. Strips of flesh cling to the spikes on the thicket.

I walk for what seems like miles, sifting through the tall stalks of grass, and lose myself in the indistinguishable greenery. Everything looks the same to me. Thick outgrowths of vegetation black out the sky. Who knows where I am. Where I'm headed. Or if I've already been here before. For fuck sakes, I could be going round in circles. This place is nothing but a maze running through the belly of the jungle.

But being lost isn't the only thing that worries me. There is something off here. I can't quite put my finger on it, but it feels bad. The jungle is dead quiet. There is no sign of life out there. I haven't seen a thing in this sprawling, breathing ecosystem. It's got no vitals showing, no pulse: no monkeys swinging from the vines, ant hills jutting the ground, or flies drawn to the stink of my decomposing body. So far as I can tell, I'm all alone.

It's strange, but whatever this place is, it does not look like home.

I fall back on the shrubbery, and take a rest. The grass feels lush and soft and almost cushions me to sleep. I check out my wrists and trace my fingers over the new scars forming around the slashes on my veins. The wounds are still fresh, and tender to the touch.

The scars remind me of the price that I have paid. The bullet wound in my head. The life I left behind, and squandered. The woman that broke my heart. The reason why I'm here. My mission to get out of hell and find the woman that sent me here.

I will never give up my chase. This blood grudge is all I have left now. It keeps me going, pumps my body full of resolve, works in lieu of a heartbeat. Lorraine won't be able to hide from me this time. She has nowhere to run. I will chase her to the ends of the world, and then hunt her down to the next.

I had nothing but love for that woman; but now whatever we used to share has gone bad. Strange how love can spoil without you even realizing it. I've never seen it last long. There's something ripe about it. It's only sweet for a moment, and always ends up turning rotten.

A cry cuts through the vegetation and brings me out from my own thoughts. It is a woman's voice. High-pitched and pleading. She calls out for help.

Something primal activates in me. I get up and run through the stalks of grass. I hone in on her, follow the sound of her crying, and try to track her down. The woman's cries grow more desperate. Her voice races. It starts to break. Gets panicked. Suddenly, she screams.

I find an open path through the grass, and run down a set of sloping hills until I reach a pond at a small clearing in the jungle. I stop in my tracks at the water's edge.

A group of women splash around in the inky pond. They swim naked on the water, basking in the light that creeps through the bush. They all cry for help in sweet, pleading tones of feminine obeisance, their melody full of glamour and allure.

The girls are pretty; rosy with color, pink nipples flush and alive. They wet their long, flowing hair, and curl their fingers at me. There's nothing hotter for the dead than the vital signs of life. Ghost tracers of adrenaline and horniness rush through me. They got me hot with lust.

The women swim seductively through the water and call out for help. One in particular draws me to her. The others just disappear for me into the background. I lock eyes with a sexy blonde in the middle of the pool. She hides her smile behind the back of her hand, and begs for my help, swooshing back and forth in the inky water. It's her: I know it. She owns the voice that I heard in the jungle; the one that got me going, and I've been chasing after.

I slosh into the pond half expecting to sink, but the water only goes up to my chest. The pond seems pretty shallow. Not the kind of depths you need rescuing from. But I ignore that, and rush in after her. I can't help it. She has some magnetic hold on me. When I reach the blonde she leaps into my arms. The girl clings close to me, her breath hot on my neck.

I swim us back to the shore, get myself out of the pond first, and then offer her my hand. The girl shakes her head. She doesn't want to leave the water. She wades in the cloudy pool, her body dipped up to the waste.

"Can a girl pay back your kindness?" she asks.

"You can go to town," I answer.

The girl grips my legs and slides my hips back into the water. She straddles on top of me, nice and snug, keeping her lower half submerged. Her lips slurp on mine, gently nibbling at my tongue. The hard thump of her racing heartbeat makes me pop an erection.

She feels wet, and I slide in easy. The girl swallows me in one take. I take her breasts in my hands and circle my thumbs on her nipples. She rides me hard, whipping her blonde hair, making me buck like a rodeo clown just to keep up with her.

I want to get a good rhythm going and fuck her hard, so I grab on to her hips, and lift her ass out of the water to change positions. My eyes go wide. I recoil and drop her back into the pond. The girl has no legs, only a wriggling white tail, ribbed like an earthworm's; the nib's covered with four corkscrewed spikes.

The blonde grips at my ankles, and drags me into the water. A cold pang shoots up my spine as I plunge into a deep tunnel that leads to a cavern at the bottom of the pond.

Skeletons and bloated bodies litter the ground, and pile up as sediment. I watch a host of millions of disemboweled corpses shift under a heap of skulls. They reach out from under the pile and try to get a hold of me, scraping at my suit with their bones.

She looms over me, swallowing water and regurgitating a trail of bubbles. I squirm, but can't get loose. The end of her tail probes between my legs, pushing against the base of my pelvis. The spikes tear into me with a painful, twisting motion and drive inside. I push her away, but she keeps thrusting into me until the spikes crack the bone.

There are other girls all around me; their tails moving in a sinew of alternating grooves. They each have a corpse of their own and are ripping them open, scavenging the entrails, feeding, and spitting out their bones.

The blonde drives her spiked tail back and forth in a sawing motion and starts gutting me open. Fuck this. I'm out. I take out the reaper's razor. The glint of the ivory handle blinds her; she covers her eyes. I take no chances and slide the blade from my wrist to the hilt of my arm.

CHAPTER TWENTY

DARK HUNGERS

Don't remember how I hit the ground this time. One too many drops on the head. Must be getting brain damage. My skull feels riddled with cracks.

The earth sinks beneath me. I can't get back on my feet—just keep splattering muck off the ground. My body feels slimed. Slick all over. Sticky ropes of this gunk dribble off of me. I keep slipping on the stuff. It gets everywhere. Sprays on my face. Oozes through the gaps in my teeth. Seeps deep into the fibers of my secondhand funerary suit, then my underwear, and socks, until it reaches and sticks between my toes.

I lie on my belly in this thin strip of land, an islet of boggy earth, surrounded by a sea of sizzling acid. A puff of fumes wafts from the vat of acid and slips up my nostrils. The stench makes me curl up into a ball. A mean burn scorches through my nasal cavities. It cooks the frontal lobes of my brain—smoke empties through the hole in the back of my head. Dizzy, I lean over the edge of the islet and hack a wad of embalming fluid.

Corpses huddle together on other small islets as the acid eats away at the coastlines. The earth crumbles apart in a slow, carbonated fizz. The waves gobble up the shores, nibbling their way to the center, driving the dead further and further from the receding edge.

Bodies pile one on top of the other. The dead fight for space in a desperate scramble to escape the acid. They go at each other with rocks and makeshift shivs, using each other's bones as bludgeoning weapons. The beaten bodies are tossed overboard. The corpses sink into the acid. Their skin burns off in a slide. Fat pops—oil spattering off a hot skillet. Half consumed skeletons scream for help.

The sea burps the remains of the dead. I get hit by a spatter of acid. The juices burn a hole through my suit. It spreads onto the skin of my arm. Every hair goes up in smoke. My skin gnarls back and exposes the muscle, then the meat just slips clear off the bone.

I spit at the wound to make it feel better, but the burning remains.

I manage to get back on my feet and take a look around this place. But it is nothing special. Just another shitty underworld.

A swarm of black flies hover over my head. They are big assed, Buick sized suckers. Red, multi-vision eyes scan the ground as they drone over the islets. The buzz of their wings sounds mechanical. They dive in and snatch the dead right off their feet, taking them into the air.

One of the flies trains its bug-eyes on me, and zips in my direction. It maneuvers quickly, zigzags from side to side, going into wild barrel rolls. The flight pattern is disorienting. Makes me dizzy. It keeps me on my toes, shifting and moving around like an idiot.

The fly head butts me smack in the gut. My wind gets knocked out, and I keel over, face first into a puddle of slime. The fly makes a roundabout turn and comes back for me. The insect buzzes closer. I can't help but shudder as it approaches. My skin flaring with goosebumps. It sinks its mandibles into the back of my neck, and lifts me off the ground.

The fly rejoins the rest of the swarm. They take their catch, and drop them into a large, communal nest. The nest is braced against these sweeping, flesh colored walls. It looks glued together out of a latticework of body parts, loose bones, and ragged balls of old clothes. All mixed in with slime as mortar.

I watch the other corpses cling to the insect's legs to avoid what they got coming. They all scream as they drop. I just close my eyes, and hold my breath like before taking a plunge in water.

The flesh fly lets go of me and I land right on top of a pile of eggs in the center of the nest. The eggs are held together into a clutch by a frothy, slick of jelly. I sink into the liquid, pushing aside the baby worms to gasp for air. The larvae shift inside the roe. I can see them move through the transparent membranes. The hatchlings wriggle and push against the egg's casing. Fat, albino rollers screeching to get out.

I make my way out of the clutch of eggs, breaking through a crust of caked blood that holds this thing together like a pie. A few of the other corpses make it out with me. The rest remain trapped inside.

I back away from the larvae, and wipe the gunk off my face. Those things get antsier inside their eggs. They look angry and caged—about to hatch. I have to find a way out of here, and get back home, before these monsters break free with an empty stomach.

Some of the stiffs make a break for it. I watch the corpses climb up the grooves in the flesh colored walls. A handful have made it all the way to the top. They collect around this puckered opening that opens and closes, letting scraps of light inside.

The larvae start popping out of their eggs. They burst through the shells: the nibs of their white tails whipping. The fat little crawlers wriggle on their bellies, sniffing around the floor, leaving behind a trail of ooze from their circular, toothed mouths—the kind made for suction feeding.

I make a run for it. The crawlers set on after me. They roll over each other, hungry and slobbering, snaking behind me. One of the larvae catches up with me. It plunges its needle point teeth into my calf, lips firm on the meat, suckling at the gush of blood.

A couple of more larvae slither on me. I feel one nestling deep into my armpit, sniffing for a soft patch of skin to latch onto. The other finds a spot near my ass.

I wave the Reaper's straight razor and flick out the blade. One of the larvae perks up and watches the steel gleam. I swipe the razor, cutting a lengthwise gash across its face, splitting its mouth into two open flaps. It screeches, and lunges at me. I slash at it again, lopping off the entire head. The larva's warm blood trickles down my face. I wipe the gunk off my eyes and pluck the parasites off me, one by one. They tear chunks of skin as their mouths peel off. I grab them from the tail, slit open their bellies, and let their innards hang.

My blood goes up—black smoke swirls in my belly. The demon inside rises. It needs to be fed. Dark hungers take me over.

I go at the rest of the nest in a fit of some mother fucking bloodlust. The larvae are fat and stupid babies. They keep coming at me, single minded, hungry and slobbering, a wriggling ball of need. I squash them under my feet. Slice through their rolls of skin. Lop off tails and heads. Gut deep into their bellies to tear out ropes of the offal inside.

Something moves underneath the egg pile. It breaks the clutch of eggs loose, and sends the gelatinous balls bouncing around on the floor of the nest. An enormous fly rises from below the batch of her eggs. It is a queen. Her head is crowned with a pronged, interlaced antennae. She drags behind her a hulking backside; a wide, child bearing badonkadonk. The queen extends her wings, takes flight, and screeches after me.

I jump on the flesh colored walls, and climb with the other stiffs, trying to reach the opening over our heads. The walls are slick. A thick mucus sticks to the surface.

We all pick up our pace as the queen approaches. She wails as she slices through the air.

I struggle, but manage to reach the exit. Everybody is trying to get through it. A crowd of corpses crowd around the slit. The hole opens and closes. It has a wet rhythm to it—the throb of a sphincter. I'm trying to clock the tempo between openings, but there is no time. I push my way through, squeeze into the slit, and slip out on the other side.

I find myself in a wet, pink tunnel, sloshing around and trying to wade through a knee-high swamp of slime. The ground moves. It gets hit with wave after wave of the shakes. It grumbles like it's churning, better yet, in the mid of a heave. I have to cling to the walls to keep steady.

Broken bones and half-dissolved body parts crunch under my feet. I follow the corpses through the tunnel. The crowd gets thicker and bottlenecks midway through. I can finally spot the mouth to the next cave beyond the mess of the crowd.

I hear screams behind me and turn back. The fly queen has slipped through into the tunnel. The bitch is relentless. She buzzes after me. The queen mows down the crowd. She chomps off a head. Impales men with her crowned antennae. Sends the corpses scattering.

I push through crowd, and run into the next cave, but it is a dead end. The queen buzzes after me and corners me against the wall.

She shrieks and lunges. I flick out the razor blade and slash at her, cutting a prong off her antennae. The queen pins me to the wall with her hairy legs, and bites a chunk off the side of my gut.

I scream more from anger than pain, and swipe at her wings next, cutting a lengthwise tear into the transparent membrane. She shrieks and rips into my shoulder with her mandibles, picking me up, and tossing me aside like a rag doll.

My body slams on the wall, and then rolls around on the ground. The razor scratch-marks the floor as I roll. Suddenly, the cave begins to move. The ground shakes. The environment seems to be reacting to me. I watch the scratches on the floor start to bleed. That is when I realize that I am inside something very much alive.

The cave comes apart—a saw of circular teeth open to a black sky. I am being rejected by my host. I can feel it want to retch. It is disgusted by my foreign presence. I am just another parasite in here. Saliva builds up all around me, and I get hocked out.

I spitball out of its mouth. My body whirls around, cannoned out into space. As I fall back down, I see the gaping maws of a gigantic three-headed worm.

I flick the steel of the straight razor, and slash my throat open as I drop.

CHAPTER TWENTY-ONE

THE FACILITY

I drop through a thick exhaust of pollution. A sprawling industrial facility built on the side of a mountain comes up below me. Rows of smokestacks and outsized cooling towers puff black smog into the air. Steel head frames brace over underground mineshafts. Cranes haul cargo from one end of the facility to the other. A track of rail runs ingrained, stitched into the very body of the mountain.

My body dunks down the crown of a smokestack. Ash burns at my eyes. I ricochet off the sides of the chimney, and land on a bulk of coal piled on a conveyer belt.

I wipe the soot from my face just as the conveyer reaches the mouth of a fire-breathing furnace. Gears move underneath me. Pistons are at work. The belt tilts and the rollers rev up, I get tossed inside the furnace with a shower of a black coals.

Flames flare all around me. Red-hot coals gleam like the sun. The light blinds me. I feel my funerary suit going up in smoke. Piping hot steam burns my skin off in strips. I get flayed from the base of the sternum down to the hip of my pelvic bone.

My body gets dumped through a shaft when the fires die out.

I land on an empty cart rolling on a stretch of rail. It takes me past a huge, rotating machine at the center of the facility. The thing looks like a generator. The rotors of three giant turbines hum as it turns. A grid of transformers and black power cables stretches out in a complicated web that disappears into the horizon.

The train travels through rails that dig into the belly of the mountain. My cart nosedives into a mineshaft, and makes a sharp turn past the cargo elevators that lead up to the head frames. The rails spiral around in loops, going through the mines, and tunnels in a winding, heart stopping rush of a rollercoaster. My cart swerves, moving faster and faster. I have to hold on to the rim to keep from going overboard.

Inside the mountain, workers shackled on either side of the rails mine for coal with pickaxes bolted onto their hands. An iron exoskeleton harnesses over their entire bodies, and coffles them together to a hard labor assembly line. The miners are all dead; nothing but corpses. Their bodies fuse with the metal of the assembly machine. Pins and nine-inch screws drill into their skeletons. Steel clamps puncture through their skin, grip on the bone, bend the right joints, and work the muscles—forcing the stiffs into the same precise, repetitive motion: raise the pick axe, smash at the rock, and then repeat.

The stiff's faces appear stitched with goggles and barbed wire muzzles that close their jaws shut. I meet their gaze, and find nothing but the same dull eyes, and pale, defeated faces. None of them have touched the light for a lifetime. They have no will to go on. The poor bastards know it already. They're going nowhere.

The machine releases a cloud of steam. A mechanical pincer reaches from the assembly line and grabs on to me. It pulls me back with the other corpses, slamming me against the rock. Shiny steel tendrils reach into my eyes and slide under the sockets. The machine stabs its pincers through my skin, reaches inside to take hold of my bones, and drill in the screws. The metal feels cold under my flesh.

I get incorporated into the machine—just another moving cog in the assembly line. The armature bolted into my bones raises my arms, bends the elbows, shifts my waste, and forces me to strike the rock. I don't have a pick axe so I bash at it with my bare hands. The machine forces me to keep repeating the same painful motion.

After a while, most of fingers get mangled into corkscrews, the meat mashed into a pulp against the rock. A few of them have already broken off. The leftover bones poke out like shivs. I already have a hole in the back of my head, an acid burn on my arm, and the skin flayed from my belly. I am coming undone like an old sack. Don't how many more underworlds I can take before I fall to pieces.

This machine has me trapped. The exoskeleton fully attaches over my body. It synchronizes my movements with the rest of the coffle of dead slaves. The assembly line has taken over.

The razor is in my jacket's pocket and out of my reach. I can't help but smile. This couldn't get any worst. This place is the shittiest kind of hell.

I have to get out of here. Lorraine is still out there, and I have to go after her. Who knows how much time I have already wasted warping from hell to hell. I have to hurry. Revenge has an expiration date. Lorraine is mortal after all.

She cannot die. Not yet. We still have a score to settle.

A red bulb blinks on the far side of the cave. The light casts a moving shadow against the rock. Something is out there hidden in the darkness.

I call for help at the top of my lungs, scraping my throat as I scream. My cries echo through the mines—I am embarrassed by the girlish sounds that reverb back to me.

The figure at the back of the cave approaches, and steps out into the light. It crawls on its four legs. The sweep of its reptilian tail lifts a cloud of dust into the air. The demon stretches up on its hindquarters to meet me face-to-face, leering at me with its black, oily eyes.

A forked tongue laps over its fangs, "Where is your muzzle and pickaxe, sub-creature?"

"I don't have any."

"Every corpse that comes into this underworld through the proper channels is issued a one-size-fits-all muzzle, and one standard issue pickaxe per afterlife. No excuses. No substitutions."

"I did not come here through the proper channels."

"You're going to be trouble for me, aren't you? Another fucking workload... Who are you? Name yourself!" the demon screeches.

"Bloom," I reveal my name like a confession.

"Bloom, Bloom..." It taps its claws on the ground, bites its lower lip, and thinks on it. "There's no Bloom assigned to this hell. You're not one of my drones. What are you doing here, sub-creature? This facility is for employees of this afterlife only. Should I call human resources? Or better yet, security?"

"Sorry," I shrug my shoulder, "I must have taken a wrong turn somewhere."

"I knew you would be trouble..." the demon mutters.

I look around at the corpses fused into the machinery, "What is this place?"

"This is just another facility, another cog in the system," it says. "The electric output of this station powers five of the nine charted hells. We all play our parts on the other side. It is the dead that power the afterlife. Our motto here is: work in this life, heaven in the next."

"There's a heaven?" I ask.

The demon rolls its eyes, "Don't get too excited. It's just an expression. The shadow world is nothing but hells."

"Am I stuck in this place now?"

"That depends on how you got here," it closes in on me. "You aren't one of those coffin riders, are you? All those shifty bastards do is bounce from hell to hell, upsetting the system, making a mess, and more work for the rest of us. They are nothing but bums. Cosmic transients. Nobody likes them. They are a great deal of trouble."

"You don't like trouble?" I smirk.

"Trouble means more work."

"Then let me go, my friend, because I'm nothing but."

"You are one them, aren't you?" Its oily eyes widen.

"Maybe…"

"How do you do it, sub-creature?"

"Do what?"

"Journey from one hell-mouth to the next?" the demon asks.

"There's no trick to it." My voice lowers, "If you let me out of this thing, I could show you."

It sighs, mouth trembling, "I have not been out this place for centuries. My mind has gone soft in this darkness. I need a vacation. To tell you the truth, I don't even remember what it's like out there. Remind me?"

"Why would you want me to tell you when you can see it for yourself? Take a coffin ride with me."

"Where would I go…?"

"You can go wherever you want. You'll be free." My words roll out thick and seductive. "As for me, I have things to do. I'm on a mission here. I am looking for a girl. A live one."

"So this is all about love?"

"Used to be. Not anymore. Things have changed. It's all about revenge now."

"All you corpses have a taste for live pussy..." he sniggers. "A piece of advice that you may choose to ignore. If you want to feel the touch of a woman so bad, there are plenty of loose body parts piling up in the bottom of the mines. Give her up, sub-creature; the dead don't mix with the living."

"Let me go, and we can both go about our business. Make a clean break of it. No paperwork." I wink at the demon.

"Deal," the demon says, pulling at a lever with its tail.

The machine turns the screws loose, and lets me go; my body drops to the ground. I dust myself off, and take the straight razor out from my pocket. The thing gleams.

"It's all in this little beauty." I dangle it in front of him. "The razor is the skeleton key to unlocking the doors of hell."

The demon drops back on all fours and swipes at me with its tail, knocking me down. It snatches the straight razor from me, and scurries away into the darkness.

I chase after it, running down the dark caverns that run through the mine. The demon is a quick, slithering fucker, and manages to gives me the slip. I search for him everywhere, going into the countless mineshafts and tunnels, checking the elevators, looking under the suspended rail tracks, and the moving gears of the assembly line.

But I get lucky. I hear its voice screeching somewhere in the distance, and follow the sound. I find it crying, beating its tail like a spoiled child. It fumbles with the razor, biting at the steel, bashing it against the walls, unable to work the spring mechanism and release the blade with its, useless, reptilian claws.

"Need some help?" I ask. "An opposable thumb, maybe?"

"Do you know how long I have been down here with nobody but the dead for company?" It starts bawling. "I can't take it anymore!"

I swipe the razor from him, "Give me that. I'll show you how it is done."

The demon's eyes pull wide open as I make the incision, and gobs of blood drip onto my shoes.

CHAPTER TWENTY-TWO

THE LAST CITY OF THE DEAD

Pilgrims and dead refugees amass around the edge of a gaping desert canyon. I sift through the mess of bodies, and mix in with the crowd. They look filthy; their bodies hunched, worn out from the heat, faces dusky from the sand. Barefoot children roam the wasteland digging out broken pieces of armor from the ground. Women busy themselves over by the cook fires, barbequing road kill on skillets made out of dented shields. Hawkers peddle ancient religious relics in a singsong, headless statues, and bones half-eaten by the desert.

The refugees have set up camp on the bare sand, on promontories of red limestone that jut out into the canyon. Makeshift tents made out of death shrouds blow in the wind like pirate sails.

A bridge sweeps over the width of the canyon and leads to the gates of a great walled city. The structure casts a cold shadow over me. A grotesque arabesque of human and animal remains, rib cages, femurs, and horned skulls, decorate the fortifications. Severed heads spiked on the edge of the ramparts look down at the crowd and babble amongst themselves.

Domed watchtowers and sharp, stilettoed turrets sweep into the sky. A giant beacon smokes on the highest tower. Dark tendrils slip from its windows and murder holes.

This place feels familiar, like I've been here before. I can't help it. It calls to me somehow. Whatever lies behind those walls has its hooks in my soul. I need to see it for myself. Stare it in the face. The demon inside of me rises.

I approach a woman sitting by the edge of the canyon. She wears a long flowing funeral veil and stares into the void. Her eyes turn on me, unblinking, sizing me up through the netting.

"If you are looking for spare change you came to the wrong woman. I'm all tapped out, and in no mood for a shake down," she says.

I look down at my suit. It's torn to pieces. Most of it burned. I must look grimy, and smell even worse.

"I'm not a panhandler," I explain, "Just new here."

She cocks an eyebrow through the netting, "I don't believe you. Do you think I kicked the bucket yesterday? I can smell a hustle."

"Why don't you go inside the city? What are you doing out here in the desert with the rest of these suckers?" I ask.

"Same thing as everybody else. Cooling my heels. Waiting to cross the bridge."

"It's right there. Why don't you just do it?"

"It does not work that way," she shakes her head. "Every corpse that wants to cross the bridge has to be judged before they are allowed passage. You must prove yourself worthy. Only the bold enter the last city of the dead."

"This hell isn't my first rodeo," I boast. "They'll let me in. I know it."

"It is not mine either." She draws back her sleeves and shows me the mess of scar tissue crisscrossing her wrists. "Try your luck. But I warn you; be careful. Don't let this canyon swallow you. Once you go in, there is no making it back out. They say something lives down there in the void. You don't want to reach bottom and find out."

I take a step on the deck of the bridge and walk it like a plank. There are no rails. I walk with my arms outstretched to keep my balance. My body teeters from side to side. Sweat pours down my back. The ride only gets hairier. The bridge warps as I move ahead, narrowing into a thin slat, a tightrope that almost disappears the closer I get to the other side.

Black winged sentinels guard the battlements of the city walls. One of them swoops down from his perch, lands on the mouth of the bridge, and blocks my way. The sentinel draws his sword. The muscles on his arms harden as he tightens his grip on the weapon. He fans out a pair of black wings in an aggressive splay, doubling his size.

The sentinel lifts the visor on his helmet. A mischievous grin cracks his boyish face. His gleaming, icy eyes scorch right through me with a cold burn. He is a reaper.

"Step no further," the reaper says. "Name yourself, and be judged."

I clear my throat, "My name is Bloom. I want to enter the last city of the dead."

He chews on his red lips, eager for a fight, and letting it show, "You think you can get through me?"

"They say only the bold can enter this place. And I'm the boldest and baddest of these chicken shit hells. I'm a coffin rider."

"Oh, I know what you are," the young reaper smiles at me. "I can smell the other underworlds off you. They call your kind hell jumpers, suicide junkies, death runners, and coffin riders, but you are nothing but fugitives that play by no rules, but your own."

"You demons threw everything you had at me and I am still standing. I already survived through the worst your hells have to offer. I have earned my ticket inside."

He looks me up and down, "You are not ready. Not yet. You haven't even finished your first lap around the nine charted hells. Come back to me when you grow some real balls and you've taken a look at the dark places that even the dead fear to explore.

"Who knows? Maybe I'll squeeze you in," he bites his lips almost seductively. "But until then, there is nowhere for you to go but down."

The deck of the bridge falls under my feet—it drops like a trap door. My body hurls into the pit. I bounce off the rock, whirling, losing all sense of direction. Below me there is nothing but a black, plunging abyss. The void. No bottom in sight. This drop feels like it's going to last for a while. Darkness swallows me whole.

I take out the razor blade again, and roll my eyes. I have done this trick one too many times already. This whole suicide thing is getting old.

Chapter Twenty-Three

The Dead Travel Fast

Black, nighttime waters spill over the horizon. I can spot nothing but ocean all around me. I brace for impact and hit the water. Another crash-landing. My body skids and rolls on the surface. The saltwater feels solid, rock hard—breaks bones with the strength of concrete.

Waves crash against me. The surf shifts with angry currents. They keep the ocean unsettled, getting progressively larger, more aggressive, swelling into a series of angry, apocalyptic tidal waves. Real deal motherfucking sea monsters.

I flail about, struggling to keep afloat, swallowing mouthfuls of tacky, acrid saltwater. And I am not alone. The ocean teems with dead bodies. They are everywhere. Corpses bob on the surface: eyes red and stinging with salt. They roll with the waves, battling it out, trying to drown each other. A mad scramble to stay above water. Only a few survive and keep afloat. The rest sink and stew underwater in a tangle of moving bodies, bloated flesh fused together into the shape of a humanoid rat king.

Something tugs at my shoe. The laces come undone, and I lose it. I look down, and try to make out what is happening through the distortion in the water. Corpses grab on to my pants, pop the seams, and rip off strips of fabric. They bring me down with them, and I get swallowed into the water.

I sink gingerly into the ocean. Time slows to a crawl. The raging storm in the surface is gone. There is no trace of it down here. Nothing but peace and quiet. A slow soothing, drift. I watch a cloud of albino bottom feeders glide on the ocean floor.

The feeling reminds me of that first time I committed suicide. An unexpected lull after the initial shock of the blast. The sweet sensation of driftwood as I eased into the bottom of the tub. An expensive indulgence—like nothing else.

I remember Lorraine looking back at me from the other side of the water. Those hearts up her neck beating as she swallowed.

I gnash my teeth. My temperature rises. Body starts to run hot again. The black smoke inside of me turns knots in my gut. Lorraine always knew how to get my blood up. One way or another. Love her or hate her, she always starts up something powerful in me. I'm tired of all this waiting around, tourist-hopping hells, wasting time, jumping around underworlds with no end in sight.

This is my moment. There will not be another. I can't wait any longer. I have to find her now.

That self-inflicted gunshot didn't just pop my death cherry: it also changed me; it made me take control of my destiny for the first time, and man up. Being dead is a better fit on me. It has made me harder, and I like it.

The straight razor slips out from my jacket's pocket, and floats away from me. I reach out for it, flick the blade, and watch a plume of blood rise to the surface.

I come to when I hit solid ground. Everything around me moves in a blur, but it slowly starts to come into focus at the edges of my periphery. My knees buckle when I try to get up. My stomach feels off. Some sort of multiple-suicide motion sickness kind of thing. I've been overdoing it. Overindulged. The flesh around my wrists already looks flayed down to the bone. This sinking feeling in my gut doesn't let up until I get on my feet and notice the crowd roaring all around me.

This time I landed in the middle of an enormous stadium, on the bloodstained sands of a coliseum. A mob of leather-faced monsters, demons, dead humans, and dark winged reapers look down on the arena from the stands. They cheer and wave their banners—drink bottle after bottle, eat cooked flesh off the bone, and toss the leftovers over the rails.

I watch a group of uniformed men in full camo gear push out a rabble of corpses from a set of underground cells. They use water hoses and smoke grenades to force them out and make them scatter about the arena.

These corpses are fresh meat. No doubt about it. Tonight's entertainment for the crowd.

All of a sudden the nosebleed seats go wild. Every stiff down in the arena starts running. The ground rumbles under my feet. A loud roar sounds off. I turn my head over my shoulder, and scream.

The things come closer; a pair of slithering, monstrous skeletons. The carcasses of undead leviathans. Monsters from the undiscovered cracks in the ocean floor. They crawl on their fossilized ribs, snapping their jaws, baring a mouthful of fangs, waving their bare-boned tails like they were still underwater. The only living tissue they have left is a pair of glowing, yellow eyeballs. They snap at the scattering bodies, scooping them into their jaws, munching on their bones, and spitting out detritus of gnarled body parts.

I back away quietly to get the hell out of here, but I bump into something. I reach back and feel warm slime run over my hands. My body shudders. There is another monster behind me: a giant, horned toad. He sits on his haunches right next to me. The toad spits out his tongue—a series of retractable chains attached to the head of a spiked mace. I duck as the weapon cannonballs over my head.

I scuff and roll on the ground. Other stiffs crawl around the sand with me, trying to lay low. The toad goes at me again, fires the flail, misses, and hits an old man standing beside me, smashing his skull flat with the steel.

The toad slurps the ball and chain back into his mouth, and releases a load burp. I have to take my chances. It is now or never. He only takes a few seconds every time to reload. I flick out the razor blade and lunge at the creature.

I run at the toad screaming, and slice through the length of his giant belly—harpoons, maces, and ropes of chains and viscera unroll from the slit and plop on the sand. The toad topples over with a groan.

I wipe the red off the blade on my pants' leg. The stadium spins around me. The noise of the crowd hits me in waves. I feel fevered. Sweat trickles down my face. My blood is up. The temperature keeps rising. Fire crackles in my veins. The sensation is too close to a heartbeat to want to let go. I like it. And I want more.

I run across the arena and jump on one of the leviathan's back. The creatures bucks around and tries to knock me off it, but I'm holding on tight. I crawl up the skeleton using the vertebrae like the rungs of a ladder. When I reach its head, I turn the straight razor around into an icepick grip and pop its yellow eyeballs. The monster crashes and shrivels in the sand, gone to another afterlife.

The other leviathan turns around and lunges at me. I try to sidestep the incoming animal, but it manages to nip at me and take a chunk off my shoulder, ripping the meat and a tangle of nerves. The wound stings, but I play through the pain. I wait until the leviathan goes at me again. This time I'm ready for it. I leap on top of its snout before it gets to me, and stab my razor into its eye sockets, driving the blade through the wet goo until it hits the skull bone.

The spectators jump to their feet and cheer. They love me. Go wild at my performance. Their banners are waving. Demons hoot and stomp their hoofed feet on the stands. Fights break out between the humans in the nosebleeds. The crowd's riled up and clapping, throwing bottles into the arena, demanding more blood.

The ground rumbles under my feet. A horde of broken down corpses burst out from the sand. Women, all of them dead. Long white hair drapes over their decomposing bodies. They are naked, almost see-through, nothing but a net of veins, and scraps of flesh on bone. The girls wail banshee-pitched and swarm at me. They pull at my clothes. Take bites at my neck. Claw at me with their sharp, blackened nails.

I swipe at them with my razor, and kick some ass. There is no art to it. Just wild, rough hacking: fingers fly off and the razor scratch marks bone. The blade hacks at them, breaks their ribcages apart, splits their jaws wide open, and scatters their teeth on the sand.

My veins pump full of hot undead plasma. Something dark masking the effects of adrenaline makes my nerve endings prickle. The rush is something else. I can feel the heat bringing my cold tissue to life again.

I was never any good at being human; never did connect with the condition. That world up there was something alien to me— its people total strangers. I was so afraid of being up there that all I wanted to do was come down here. But something has changed in me. I look at the gore all around me, the massacre I have just committed, the blood on my hands, and realize these hells fit me better than the world off the living ever did. Down here I have come into my own. Bloomed. I am a far better demon than a random, simple human.

The spectators topple over each other and cheer from the stands. But playtime is over. I'm nothing if not a good showman. I leave them wanting more. I take the straight razor and place it against my throat. The stands go quiet. Tension thickens. The spectators are on the edge of their seats. I smile, and cut into my neck until I snap the spine and my head lops off and rolls on the sand. The crowd goes nuts.

《《——》》

Colored rings stretch across a whirling, unforgiving sky as I enter the atmosphere. Thunder roars above me. I'm in the middle of a hell of a storm. My body whips about, spinning, picking up speed. There is no place to land, no solid ground, only a roiling world made out of clouds of concentrated nitrogen and methane gasses.

The giant stone, totem of an albino worm rises from the eye of the storm.

Other corpses fly around in circles with the storm. Their bodies blur into static. Distorted like ghosts. Streaks of movement. The stiffs move too quickly for my eyes to focus on them. I see the faces I want to see reflected on their bodies. Lorraine and the heart shaped tattoos that run up her neck. The Sybil and her mole. Leroy taking off his sunglasses. The black winged reaper eyeing me through his binoculars. But they are not real, just mirages. Glitches of the brain. My mind turning on itself.

I am tired of drifting through the underworld. My body feels wrecked, shocked. My mind can't be far behind. Hell jumping is an open door invitation for going insane. It's taking its toll; changing me. The longer I stay here, the more I feel like this is where I really belong.

But I shake off these crazy thoughts. I'm on a mission here. The clock is ticking. I have to get the fuck out of hell, and find her. I flick the razor loose, kiss the curve of the scythe-shaped blade, and close my eyes.

You brought this on yourself. I had no choice. I didn't want to stop feeling for you. I wanted to keep our connection alive. A cycle of vengeance and betrayal is all that binds us now. And maybe that's enough. Cheap replacement for love, I know, but it does the trick and fills up the hollow inside.

Do you know that I am coming? Are you afraid? Be careful, my love, for the dead travel fast.

Chapter Twenty-Four

Playing Dead

I appear in the middle of a vast, arctic tundra, trekking through the snow. Nothing ahead and nothing behind. This place looks like another dead end.

The wind cuts through my skin and has got me shivering. Frostbite already nibbles at my toes. I flick my jacket's collar out of habit, but it does nothing to help me weather the cold. My body aches all over. I stumble around exhausted. Every breath feels labored. My joints get harder to bend. Fingers cripple into a claw. I suddenly collapse into the snow

I can feel it in my bones. The cold is creeping in. Freezing my body solid. Weighing me down. This place is going to be my grave. My new home. I am never getting out of here.

Something moves in the distance. I cup my hands over my eyes like a visor. It starts as a distortion in the white background, but it slowly comes into focus. Riders. I spot a group of figures moving in a mounted caravan a few miles away. They seem to be coming from the direction of the abandoned, snow-covered ruins of an ancient citadel.

I slog through the snow, climb to the top of a nearby hill, and yell out, "Hey, over here!"

The caravan stops at the sound of my voice. Riders dismount from their animal's backs. The men's thick, hulking furs flap with the wind currents. They form a circle around the rest of their party, and seem to be staring right at me, sizing me up. A group of them draws rifles and assumes a firing stance. Their bodies tilt in my direction, weapons cocked high, butts on the nooks of their shoulders. I hear the sound of their pump action rifles loading a round of slugs just for me.

The men open fire. Bullets pepper the ground. They shoot and zip right through me. The slugs lodge into my gut, drill through my organs, and go right out the back. The riders reload, and take aim at me again. I make a run for it as a fresh round of bullets go off.

My body rolls down the hill. I scurry off on my hands and knees, gradually getting on my two feet, taking wide, desperate strides to find a hiding place in this barren wasteland. My head cranes back: the riders buck on their animals, whipping the reigns, trotting at full speed, and gaining ground on me.

I plow through the snow and make my way down a steep, rolling slope that leads down to a frozen lake. I look around for places to hide. There are a series of caves dug into the snow at the far end of the ice. I run inside the nearest cave, and press my back against the wall.

It is dark in here. Icicles pyramid from the ceiling, sharp like fangs. I wet my finger inside my mouth, touch the ice, and watch it stick. A small mischief that I have always indulged myself with since I was a kid.

I sink into the darkness of the cave. The riders could still be out there. I crouch down, clasp my hands over my mouth, and go quiet. Holding my breath. Not daring to move a muscle. Showing no signs of life. Still like the grave.

"Playing dead?" Laughter reverbs throughout the cavern.

The reaper strikes a match and fires up a cigarette, lifting the darkness from the cave. He leans back on the wall with his ankles crossed. His white suit is impeccably pressed, the line of his jacket looks crisp, sharp, and could probably cut glass. A star-nosed mole nuzzles in his arms. He runs his fingers on the animal's albino fur, and smiles as the little guy squirms.

"Well? Tell me, Mr. Bloom, how do you like your coffin ride so far?"

"This place only gets worst the deeper I go."

"In a way, you are a very lucky man. Not many souls have the chance to visit the nine charted hells."

"I've seen enough," I mutter.

"Poor fool, you haven't seen anything yet," the old man blows a thin stream of smoke, knives at my eyes. "You have only scratched the surface of what these hells have to offer. There are a whole host of horrors out there."

"Believe me, I've had my fill. Is there no place out there that gives the dead some peace and quiet?"

"No," he says it without emotion, shrugging his shoulders.

"You lied to me," I pull out the razor blade and wave it in his face. "You said this thing could bring me back home."

"Is that what I said?"

"No..." I admit, "you said I could try my luck at it."

"Ah...so I made no promises, after all."

"But you implied it. Now I am lost here. You tricked me!" I scream.

The albino hairs on the mole's back bristle. It turns its star-nosed snout and hisses at me. The old man coos at the animal, and manages to calm it down.

"You get tricked easily, don't you? I would have hoped you had gotten wise by now," he chuckles. "Who is really the flawed man; the liar or the sucker that falls for it?

"All this time you have only fooled yourself, Mr. Bloom. It's all on your shoulders; no else's. Take some responsibility for once. You have been running from something for your entire life, never facing the moment, always on the escape, one bullet, and wrist slash after the next. Time to man up, boy."

I don't say anything. He cuts me to the quick. The old man is right. I did nothing but run away from my problems when I was living. I was a bad fucking escape artist. That first suicide was the natural progression of my lifelong quest to hide from the world.

The old man might be right, but I can't let him see it. I've always been petty that way. I toss the razor at him like a spoiled child.

"I have to get home," I keep repeating the same tired line, over and over.

He shakes his head, disappointed, "This is all about that live girl, isn't't? Your great obsession."

I nod my head.

"To tell you the truth," he says. "You're not the first corpse with an obsession for live tail. In fact, you all seem to have an inclination for them."

"I need to get back to her. This isn't my home. I don't belong here," I mutter.

"Are you sure about that?"

"What do you mean?"

"Something happens to men who have been out here too long, jumping from one hell to the next. This place changes them.

125

It's the sights and smells of death: the very fabric of the underworld, the particles of black matter. They peel back the skin and reveal the monsters underneath. Nothing that stays here long enough is ever the same again. It happens every time, slow but sure. We adapt to this harsh environment, and sooner or later become just another devil lost in hell.

He turns his icy eyes on me, "Once upon a time, I wasn't very different than you. It hurt like a bitch when I dropped."

The reaper slips his fingers in his mouth and mimics the barrel of a gun going off. The old man takes off his Panama hat, and reveals the bullet wound in the back of his head.

He leans closer to me, nodding, sharing a familiarity, "Do you feel it yet…the change?"

I feel it in the marrow of my bones. Hot bloodlust burns through me. The demon in the blood. The reaper has my number. I've been feeling it happen, bubbling up inside of me. The rush from violence. My escalating suicides. The call from the city of the dead. The cloud of smoke beating inside of me. This change has already taken hold of me.

It frightens me how much I like it, so I lie to him, and I think he knows it, "No. I feel nothing."

The reapers puts the mole on the ground and picks up the straight razor. He fingers the ivory handle and flicks out the blade.

"Do you want me to send your ungrateful carcass back home?"

"Yes," I gnash my teeth, "Lorraine and I are going to be together again just like we planned."

"What's so special about this girl anyway?"

"A lot of love gone bad."

The reaper stubs out his cigarette, and the cave goes black, "I am disappointed in you. I mistook you for a different sort: the kind of man who could find his place guarding the battlements of the last city of the dead, fully armored, striking fear with a pair of deadly shade wings. This underworld could have been yours to reap. But you are not ready. Not yet. You still have to let go, and find your place in the shadows.

"So, let's have some fun and indulge this sick, twisted obsession of yours," The reaper slashes my throat, and sends me packing to the next world.

CHAPTER TWENTY-FIVE

HOME

The upward pull makes my gut crawl into itself—insides turned into a deep, sinking hollow. I lie flat on the ground, cheek pressed against the checkered linoleum. A low ding goes off as the elevator's doors slide open.

I step out of the elevator car into a badly lit, narrowing hallway. Fluorescent lights flicker unsteadily as I go by. My shoes drag on the carpet, grazing against the shag, building up friction, charging my body with an electric static.

The glow of television screens oozes from the gaps between the doors and the floor. Strange eyes look out from behind the fastened chains. This guy up ahead rides his girl's skirt up her thighs and slams her with a kiss against the wall. An old man smokes shirtless outside his doorway. He wears tinted glasses for his cataracts, and doesn't even notice as I walk by and brush his shoulder.

None of them notices me. Nobody really pays attention. They gloss over me with empty, faded eyes. Lost in their own lives. Blind to what is right in front of them. I almost want them to see me, to make a connection, acknowledge each other's number, and avoid the creep of loneliness for one small moment.

But the living got no time for the dead.

This place feels strange, but there is something familiar about it. It replays in slow motion in my head. The memory cloudy. This is only an echo of what I remember. An old movie with bad definition. The ruins of a forgotten world. Each step I take feels like going backwards.

I can't believe it; I'm back home.

I walk to the end of the hallway, and reach the door to our old apartment. My eyes close as I knock my head against the frame. Old memories rush back to me living and breathing. They swell up, painful, building up pressure in my head. I place the flat of my hand on the wood, and feel warmth coming from the other side.

Something holds me back. I rest on the balls of my feet, hesitant to claim what I came here for. But I cannot stop. There is no going back now. Things have already been set in motion. I have to reach the end this road I'm on. It is time to finish this. I force the door open, and walk inside.

Even in the dark, I remember the layout of the apartment perfectly. This place was once my home. I move through it on autopilot. Every inch mapped out from memory. I spent so much time here. This space felt like my very own. The familiarity brings a smile to my face. The fridge hums and rattles like always. Dirty dishes pile up in the sink. Empty takeout bags slump on the kitchen counter.

This place has a warm, cozy vibe, a hint of a stale smell. There's no mistaking it; I'm finally home.

It feels strange to walk through the left overs of my life. I check out my old spot on the sofa, where I used to curl and nap on Sundays. The groove of my body still indents the cushions.

An old charger of mine that fit Lorraine's phone is slotted into the light socket. I peer into the fish bowl she gave me for my birthday; it is still empty, the fish died on that very same day, and no one ever bothered to replace it.

But what really strikes me, hits me sledgehammer hard in the gut, is all the things that are missing. Everything of mine that has just disappeared. Gone without a trace. Or up in smoke. Buried away in a dumpster, just like me.

I pass by the bathroom and can't help but peep inside. It calls to me. The allure of the scene of an old crime. Memories bubble up in a rush, fresh and real as the moment itself: my first kill. The door creaks open. I step inside and almost slip on the wet floor. The sink's exposed piping never did stop leaking.

It looks like Lorraine just took a bath. The tub's sucks the remaining suds down the drain. A dank, crumpled towel curls up in the corner like a tired, aging bloodhound. Steam clings to the air, and fogs up the mirror. I wipe the surface clean, and search for my face in it, but nothing reflects back to me.

I wave my hands in front of the mirror, and again, nothing. A cold, sinking feeling reaches into the pit of my stomach. My head shakes. This feels fucking unreal. I don't want to believe it. I keep on mumbling the same thing, "No way."

This is too creepy. I get the hell out of there.

Out in the hall, one polka-dotted white pump stands upright on its kitten heels; its match, lies strewn over on its side a few feet away. Lorraine's clothes form a trail of bread crumbs that leads into our old bedroom. I follow the traces she leaves behind: her rumpled remains, the shedded skin. A zippered mini lies on top of a pile of laundry. Knee-length stockings hang off the doorknob. An emptied tumbler makes a wet ring on her dressing table; her lipstick stains the rim red. I don't linger on the brazier slung over the mirror; my lack of reflection takes me to a bad place.

I spot flesh-colored panties at the foot of the bed, and pick them up by the thin elastic thong. They are the end of the road. She is good and cornered.

Lorraine stretches sluggishly on the mattress. She lies on her belly. Legs tangled between the sheets. The meat of her thighs, her warm instep, clamped vice-tight on the camber of her pillow. Her face hides playfully behind thick, ropes of yellow hair.

I sit next to her on the bed, and watch her sleep like I used to do when we were together. Lorraine's body heaves as she breathes. Heart beats, and pumps her full of fresh oxygenated blood. Her cheeks go flush. Lips part, red, wet, and alive.

I can't help stroke her yellow hair, and brush it off her face: the heart-shaped tattoos running up her jugular panic and beat faster when exposed. Looking at her lying there sleeping, dreaming, in a mid-state, practice run between life and death, I remember why loving her was so easy for me.

My blood goes hot with lust. I lunge at her, but stop midway. All I want to do is collapse on top of her. Give her a kiss. But I decide against risking the intimacy, and whisper into her ear instead, "Lorraine...can you feel it? We're together again. There is nowhere to run. I've got you now."

Lorraine's eyes shudder open. They bulge big and wide, wet with fear. She scans the room through the darkness, and looks right through me. Lorraine can't see me, but she can feel that I'm close. She reacts to the spectral reverb of my voice, the warped screeching that spills out of the mouths of the dead.

Her reaction to me, this blind fear at the monster at her side, only makes me hotter. Dark, roiling demons deep in my guts claim over me. They split my mouth into a twisted snigger.

The spell comes natural, a thing of instinct, I know exactly what to do. I focus on the dark cloud roiling inside of me and watch the nibs of his fingers displace and spread out in a swirl of smoke. The tendrils stretch out and pierce through her skin—driving through the meat and bone, hooking into her very core.

Tears stream down her face. She tries to scream. I clamp her mouth shut and pin her to the bed. My forearm braces her neck. I spread open her legs as the black smoke drives deeper into her body.

An electric charge builds up in the room. The atmosphere is thick with it. I can feel it sparking up against my body. The TV powers on, grainy with static. The drawers of the dresser open and close back shut. The light bulbs explode. A large crack bisects the entire length of the mirror on the dresser, and breaks it in half. Shadows melt and spill on the floor, pooling around the legs of the bed.

She resists me with everything she's got; teeth gritted, bucking and trashing against me, trying to throw me off. I turn her on her back and claw at her flesh, raking away strips of meat, digging deeper, breaking through to the sternum, ramming my fist into her chest cavity until my fingers grip around her beating heart. The black tendrils spread through her veins and arteries, taking root, anchoring to the marrow on her bones.

Lorraine clenches her body to stop me from getting inside, but it is too late. My hooks are already in. I got her now.

I push harder, tearing at the ligatures, and slip into her body. It's snug in here. Pressure builds up in my skull as my head goes in. I rip into her entrails, move things around, and nestle myself in the wet space. She lets loose a horrible cry.

Lorraine's body roils on the mattress, bending at crooked angles, joints stiff and graceless. She arches her back and contorts into a rawboned, arachnid crabwalk. Her nails dig into the sheets like claws. Black smoke slips from her lips. Our shared eyes roll back to the whites, and her body lifts from the sheets, and hovers above the bed.

My face hides under her skin. Lorraine starts to fades away. The shadow cast from her body is not her own. I suck breath through her mouth and make the possession complete. I leech off her. Her chest expands, and I piggyback off her breathing. We share the same air now, and I use up more than my fair share. With every breath I get bolder, keeping more and more for myself. Soon there will be nothing left for her.

I blink her eyes open and awaken to the world again, rasping a painful breath through her throat. Dark, smoky tendrils ooze out of my ghost flesh and fuse with her nerve endings. Our bodies connect at the spine. We start sharing the same racing heartbeat.

But something doesn't feel right. I notice a creeping sensation in the back of our shared body. A chemical build up that explodes into our bloodstream. The smell is strong and metallic. Wave after wave of the stuff pulsates through us: the thick, contagious pheromones of fear.

It fucking consumes everything. I can feel nothing else. The fear beats thick and aggressive, arousing the nerves and goose bumping the flesh, making me feel painfully alive. Our wheezed breathing becomes stalled, and hyperventilated. Heart rates race. Veins pop close to bursting, swelling with blood pressure. The spray of warm piss drips down the curve of our thighs.

Ever since I died I've chased after something like the high of being alive, but I can't seem to handle the real experience, it is too much for me. I do not like this I'm feeling. Not one bit. I had forgotten what it was like to be human. How bad it can get. The animal fear is always there, festering inside of you, even if you don't know it. It is a biological condition of living. It has been a long time since I have felt this afraid, this alive. I want to shake the feeling off me, but I can't. It sticks to me.

My skin grows sensitive, crawling with microscopic dust mites, and bacteria. I can feel every individual strand of hair. The movement of balls of meshed food in our shared bowels. Body fluids that seep out from every orifice.

I can't take it anymore. I can feel myself aging. The slight, almost imperceptible screams of thousands of cells dying, cellular integrity collapsing, and slowly poisoning the rest of the body. The tickle of decay is disgusting; the growing stink even worse. I never felt more alien to this world than I do now, at this moment. The slimy biology of living feels repulsive. Death seems so much cleaner.

The anger inside of me wanes. Her betrayal loses some of its sting. Her pain does not satisfy what I crave for. I don't get any sense of retribution. This gesture feels empty. Like it doesn't mean a thing. This whole revenge thing isn't really doing it for me anymore. Payment doesn't balance the scales. What's done is done. The guilt here is shared, anyway.

It's always the same isn't? The moment never lives up to the expectation.

Lorraine might deserve my revenge, but I gain nothing from dishing it out. We are worlds apart now. The divide has grown too wide. This is not my place anymore. It stopped being my home a long time ago, but I have been too stubborn to realize it.

I am no longer human. Hell turned me into something else: the gloomy shadow of death.

Lorraine and I are nothing but ghosts to each other. Painful memories of some other life. Our moment is in the past and gone. Maybe it's time for us to say goodbye after all this time.

Besides, her time will come. We can always haunt each other in hell for an eternity.

So I just let her go. I unhook my dark tendrils from her bones, and slip out of her. Lorraine's body bounces back on the bed. She gasps for air, drifting off into a deep sleep; the kind inhabited by nightmares that linger.

I touch her blonde hair one last time, and think about snipping one of the ends as a souvenir of our time together, but I decide against it. We both need this clean break from each other. I mouth my goodbye without saying it out loud.

I shut the door on my way out of her apartment, and walk down the long stretch of hallway. Inside the elevator, I press the button to the ground floor, low as I can go. I lean back and stick my hands inside my pockets: there's something inside—the reaper's razor blade.

The sheen of its ivory handle blinds me. I flick out the blade one more time, making it sing as it slices the air. A playful smile cuts across my face like I'm getting away with something. The call of the shadow world is strong, and seduces me back home.

I catch my reflection on the gleaming blade, a pair of black wings mirror back at me.

James W. Bodden is the author of the novels the *Red Light Princess*, and *Coffin Riders*. He's down in some dank Cold War bunker, helmet on, and braced for impact.

Made in the USA
San Bernardino, CA
17 July 2015